"Don't suppose you remember me."

His drawl still apparent, the words stung rather than caressed.

Justine almost laughed out loud at the foolishness of his statement. Instead, she hid her face in the shadows.

"Luke Butler," he said with a dip of his head.

Sunlight teased the planes of his rugged face and illuminated eyes that were the deep blue-green of still water in an East Texas lake. Curling her fingers into tight fists, Justine expelled a quick breath.

"I know," she said. Painfully she groped for words while he measured her with a stare that held more than a little contempt. "I remember," she added when their gazes met.

"I wasn't sure you would."

For a moment, she thought she saw discomfort flash across his face. His lips tilted slightly into a weak smile, and he shook his head.

"You're exactly like I remembered," he said.

Instantly, she became the same nobody she'd been twenty years ago, the nobody to whom Luke Butler had mysteriously bestowed his precious attention. Even now, at the ripe old age of thirty-six, she felt the butterflies begin to rise in her stomach as the silence between them lengthened.

KATHLEEN Y'BARBO is an award-winning novelist and sixth-generation Texan. After completing a degree in marketing at Texas A&M University, she spent the next decade and a half raising children (four) and living with her engineer husband in such diverse places as Lafayette, Louisiana; Port Neches, Texas; and Jakarta, Indonesia. She now lives with her nearly grown brood near Houston, Texas, where she is active in Fellowship of The Woodlands Church as well as being a member of American Christian Romance Writers, Romance Writers of America, and the Houston Writers' Guild. She also lectures on the craft of writing at the elementary and secondary levels.

You Can't Buy Love

Kathleen Y'Barbo

Heartsong Presents

This book is lovingly dedicated to those brave women who have made the difficult choice to allow someone else to raise the children the Lord gave them (Deuteronomy 30:19). God bless you!

In addition, I would like to thank DiAnn Mills, Martha Rogers, and Myra Johnson, the lovely ladies of Seared Hearts, and also my pal Rhonda Stanley, for abundant love, laughter, and sisterhood in Christ. Without the four of you, this book would never have happened.

Finally, all my love to "The Girls from PNG": Janis Griner Blizzard, Lindell Lee Brown, Jane Tamplin Burnap, Lisa Jones Dutton, Cindy Evans Morris, and Carleen Simon. You believed in me before I believed in myself.

A note from the author:
I love to hear from my readers! You may correspond with me by writing:

Kathleen Y'Barbo
Author Relations
PO Box 719
Uhrichsville, OH 44683

ISBN 1-58660-525-9

YOU CAN'T BUY LOVE

All Scripture quotations are taken from the King James Version of the Bible.

Cover illustration by Victoria Lisi and Julius.

PRINTED IN THE U.S.A.

prologue

For I am persuaded, that neither death, nor life,
nor angels, nor principalities, nor powers,
nor things present, nor things to come, nor height, nor depth, nor any other creature, shall be able to separate us from the love of God, which is in Christ Jesus our Lord.
ROMANS 8:38–39

A man's heart deviseth his way:
but the LORD *directeth his steps.*
PROVERBS 16:9

Luke eased off the Harley beside the sign that read "Kiwanis welcomes you to Bailey's Fork." He slapped at the fronts of his thighs to shake off the road dust. From where he stood, he could almost see the whole town of Bailey's Fork, Texas.

Over there would be the high school and the football field that he once thought was the center of the world. He laughed, just a little, at the thought. If only life could be made good and whole again by the scoring of a touchdown or the satisfying crunch of a tackle.

But life wasn't football, not anymore.

Luke shook his head. Even then, when he could light up the scoreboard every Friday night without fail, football had taken a backseat to a pretty blue-eyed high school sophomore named Justine Kane. She'd been his for a brief while, and while it lasted, life had been good. Football only made living interesting, and later, profitable.

When Justine told him to get lost, he'd taken her seriously and done just that. He got out of town, away from Justine and the shame of having her tell him his plans for the rest of his life didn't quite measure up to hers.

She'd been wrong, of course. Luke Butler had measured up more than adequately, even after the body he'd trained for football turned against him.

Luke squinted against the glare of the midafternoon sun and raised a hand to his brow. In his life there had been a whole lot of wins and only one loss that counted. With the end chasing him like a three-hundred-pound lineman, there was just one more thing he had to do before he could head for the bench.

He threw a leg over the Harley and cranked it. With a wicked grin and a loud whoop, he kicked the big, mean machine into gear and rode into town the same way he'd ridden out twenty years ago.

Like he owned the place.

one

"I heard he owned the place. Luke Butler, that is."

Abby Kane Meyer let the faded red-and-white-checked curtain fall back into place and turned her back on the window that held the best view of First Street and the First National Bank of Bailey's Fork. "The famous Mr. Butler's bought nearly every piece of property in this town that was for sale."

She paused, a rare thing for one so vocally gifted and stubbornly opinionated. "He'll be after you next, Blondie," she continued, one auburn eyebrow lifted.

Justine Kane, younger by four years but, to her own mind, wiser by decades, handed her the last of the old hymnals without comment. Her imagination flitted toward her sister's warning, then shut down, a trained response to a period of her life better left unvisited.

"I'll call the relief society and let them know we've got more for them," she said with a smile that trembled at the corners. "We're almost done."

Her sister threw the hymnals in the box and closed it with a flourish, creating a dust cloud that sent them both into a fit of coughing. When the smoke screen settled, their gazes met.

Abby frowned. "Stop being well adjusted for a minute and listen to me."

"Can we not talk about this? He—" After twenty years, Justine still couldn't speak his name aloud. "—is ancient history."

Abby shook her head. "Ancient but not forgotten."

"No," Justine said. "Not forgotten, but definitely finished."

How could she forget? She saw the man every time she looked at the picture on her mantel. Still, what little the two of them shared so long ago had ended the day he left Bailey's Fork. His return meant nothing more than a temporary inconvenience.

"Well, well, well," Abby said, throwing a stinging sideways look her way. "Finished, is it?"

Justine nodded and continued her work without comment. In the decade since Abby had returned to Bailey's Fork, a widow with four children, Justine had learned less was more when it came to the feisty redhead. Abby meant well, but even a saint would tire of her endless commentary and boundless knowledge. Thank goodness most of her wisdom was dispensed while she worked as a checker at the Mayfair Grocery Market. No doubt she handed out priceless nuggets of information with every item she scanned.

"I bet you'll forget all about 'finished' the first time you lay your baby blues on Mr. Butler." Abby's face brightened. "Eli saw him on ESPN the day he gave his big retirement interview."

"I thought you were dating Hugh Hawthorn."

She waved away the statement and kept on talking. "Eli told me Luke looks like a movie star. One of those movie bad guys or something." A smile bloomed. "A real rugged sort."

Justine began to hum, a time-honored way to tune out her older sister.

"While you're playing *Amazing Grace* over there, why don't you hum a few bars of *Wild Thing*, because that's what Melbalene Cotton, the new stylist at the Clip and

Curl, said he looked like on the poster she's got hanging in the back room."

Justine hummed louder. "Don't talk like that," she said when she finished. "It's wrong."

"Good thing you and I took that CPR class over at the Y last month," Abby said with a chuckle.

"What are you talking about now?"

She smiled. "Well, with Luke Butler back in town, he's likely to short circuit a few hearts."

Holding up both hands, Justine shook her head. "Abby! Enough! This is a church building for goodness sake!"

"This used to be a church building. Before the congregation moved to the new building and Mr. Wild Thing bought the place."

Justine slapped at the dirt on her jeans. "You didn't tell me he bought the old church building too." She paused. "And stop calling him that. It's not right."

"Well, I'm not exactly sure he did buy it, but he went on a buying spree last month. I heard he bought enough real estate to put all five of Bob Biggsworth's kids through college."

"The real estate agent? Very funny."

Abby gathered the end of a garbage bag into a knot and pushed it aside. "Who else but Butler would want an old brick building smack dab in the middle of town?"

"Could be anybody," Justine said with a shrug, forcing her breathing to come in a slow and measured pace.

"Could be." Abby gave Justine her smug, older-sister smirk. "Who else would come back to town with wads of cash to show a certain blond-haired, blue-eyed former girlfriend she did the wrong thing by giving him the heave-ho?"

"It wasn't like that, and you know it." Justine wiped the dust off the face of her watch and checked the time. "It's almost lunchtime. Why don't you go on home? I'll finish up here."

"Kids don't get home until three-thirty and it's my day off." Abby shrugged. "I've got all afternoon. Let's get this job done, get cleaned up, and have a late lunch next door."

They went back to work, and a silence fell between them. Unfortunately, Abby chose to break that silence with a sarcastic chuckle and a toss of her head.

"What?" Justine asked.

"I heard he rides a Harley now." She upped the wattage on her smirk. "A black one."

Justine expelled a long breath and gave Abby a hard look. "Okay, I get it. You're not going to stop until you get a reaction from me. Well, here it is. I am very happy he has done well for himself. I'm also very happy he has chosen to share some of his wealth with the community where he spent his childhood."

"You really think that's what it is? That he's just as goody-goody as you are?"

"So that's what I am?" Justine asked, working up an anger her mind knew was misplaced. "If loving the Lord and serving Him is being a goody-goody, then I'm proud to call myself one."

"Oh, come on," Abby said slowly. "I didn't mean to hurt your feelings. I love the Lord too. It's just. . ."

She paused and let the words remain unsaid. Fifteen years ago, Justine had returned to Bailey's Fork to help her father care for their ailing mother. It had been a temporary situation; just a few months and she'd be back at college pursuing the master's degree she'd begun in social work.

Somehow the months had turned to years. Her mother passed on, and her father, bless his helplessly male self, refused to manage on his own without her. In the end, the years had turned into a decade and a half, and the urge to leave had gradually faded and disappeared.

"It's not so bad being a church secretary, you know." Justine mustered a weak smile. "In fact, I rather like my job."

"But your dreams, Honey. Remember when you used to talk about doing something meaningful with your life? Remember your plans to make a difference?" Abby nudged the box with the toe of her sneaker and looked away. "Things could have been so different for you. If only. . ."

Her voice faded to nothing, again leaving unsaid what they both knew too well. If only. . .

Justine feigned excitement. "Hey, I get first peek at the topic of Pastor's weekly message."

"Oh yeah, let me know if that job ever comes available," Abby said with a chuckle. "Lord knows my aching feet could use a rest, and I just might be able to give Dave Mills a little friendly advice with the sermons."

"Abby, that's not—" A squeal of tires and the roar of an ancient car engine cut short Justine's comment. "Miss Emma's racing home to watch her stories. It must be noon."

Her sister checked her watch and nodded. "Yep, you can set your clock by the old gal. The way she comes zooming down First Street, it's a wonder Eli Watts hasn't taken her driver's license away from her."

"Then who would drive the bookmobile?" Justine asked.

Abby chuckled. "I guess you're right. It's not like there's ever anyone to hit anyway."

Justine reached for another hymnal. "That's true. I don't know why they bother to keep a light on First Street. Miss Emma's usually the only one on the road that time of day."

"Maybe that's because the rest of us stay out of her way."

The pair shared a laugh and went back to work in

earnest. In record time, they had boxed all the old hymnals and bagged most of the trash.

Justine began to hum again. She busied her hands with marking boxes while her mind wanted to race. Barely, she held it at bay.

"Seriously," Abby finally said, "what are you going to do when you see Luke again?"

What would she do? The idea of carrying on a conversation with Luke Butler was just too painful to consider.

What would she say? *It's been a long time. Oh, by the way, back in high school we made a baby together.*

"Justine?"

"Sorry." She stuffed the hymnals into an open box and reached for the packing tape. "What did you say?"

"Nothing you'd want to hear," Abby said, appraising Justine with eyes that knew too much. "Look, I'm just worried about you, that's all. You're going to run into him sooner or later, and you need to be prepared for that."

"I managed just fine when Brian found me," she said, remembering for a moment the shock she felt last spring when the call had come. Within moments, shock had given way to relief and, over the past few months, relief had turned to a love she thought she'd given up with her son. If only she could let someone besides her sister and her newfound son know of that love.

For many reasons, chief among them her concern over how the citizens of Bailey's Fork would treat her son—and her—Justine had kept silent and settled for a few brief visits and many, many phone calls. With Brian away at college in Houston, the arrangement had so far gone well.

"Seems as though you're worrying too much," Justine said. "I'm not sixteen anymore, Abby."

"I know, but—"

"But don't borrow trouble. Isn't that what Dad used to say?"

Abby smiled. "He still does, but he forgets what that means now."

"Alzheimer's disease is like that, you know," Justine said with a sad smile. "Very little of what he says makes sense."

"Maybe so, but sometimes he makes more sense than you."

Justine shook her head. "What're you talking about now?"

Abby stomped her feet and pointed a finger at her, sending thousands of fine white particles into a whirlwind. "Seems as though we have a case of denial here."

Biting back her first response along with a sneeze, Justine took a deep breath and let it out so slowly her head went faint for a moment. Then she remembered to breathe. "I'm not in denial," she finally said. "Now pass the garbage bags. I'm out."

"Then say his name." Abby dropped to her knees beside Justine and offered a warm smile. "You can't, can you?"

"Whose name?" She looked past her sister to the red-checked curtains on the window and began to hum.

Abby leaned over and slipped an arm around her shoulder. "Honey, it's all right. You've got a lot to forget." She frowned. "And a lot to lose."

Justine rocked back on her heels and drew her knees to her chest. Tiny pinpoints of worry prickled the skin at the back of her neck and danced a jig down her spine. She swatted at them, waving a hand through the dust-choked air as if removing them were as easy as slapping mosquitoes on a summer evening or brushing away flies at the Dixie Café next door.

Luke Butler was back.

Those words produced a strong physical sensation in her every time she dared give them thought. Justine knotted her fingers together and held them in her lap to keep the trembling from giving her away. Now that he'd returned, how long could her secret be safe?

"Justine?"

She snapped her head in the direction of the sound. Abby now stood at the attic door with the box of hymnals in one hand and a pair of garbage bags in the other.

"Yes?" she managed as she wiped at a streak of thick grime on her arm.

"Justine, Luke Butler is back and, unless I miss my guess, he's back for you."

She continued to work on the spot on her arm. "I don't think so."

"Oh, come on." Abby let the garbage bags drop and placed one hand on her hip. "Do you honestly think a man like that is going to come back to a place like this for no reason?"

Daring a glance in Abby's direction, she quickly looked away when their eyes met. "He has a reason. This is his home."

"No, it's not. Coral Jo down at the cleaners told me old Luke bought the folks who took in Adam a big house on the beach with a swimming pool and a cabana. Guess that'd be the closest thing he has to family." She opened her mouth, then clamped it shut. "I'm sorry, Honey," she said a moment later. "I mean the closest ones he knows about. Brian would be the closest of all since he's—"

"You said he bought them a nice house?" Justine asked, trembling inside as she faked nonchalance.

Abby nodded. "Can you feature it? A house in your backyard just for showering off after you get out of the pool. Must be nice. With four kids, I'd just be happy with my own bathroom."

Justine reached for another empty box and began piling hymnals inside. Working, even something as mindless as cleaning out the attic of the old church building, always gave her solace. She continued to move her hands, making progress at the same speed Abby made conversation—very quickly.

"Luke's brother died a couple of years ago," Abby announced.

Stunned, Justine dropped the hymnal, narrowly missing her big toe. "Adam? You're kidding. I never heard that."

Abby shook her head. "Me, either, but then I guess there wasn't any reason for us to know. Luke didn't exactly leave any friends here, and Adam wasn't much older than my boys when he went to live with that family over in Grimes County."

Vague memories of long ago bobbed near the surface. The death of Luke's mother had left the Butler boys to their own devices. Barely eighteen, Luke made a home for them by working after school and on weekends at the country club to provide for himself and his ten-year-old brother.

Then her father turned them in.

After the authorities took Adam, Luke had become cold and vindictive with a penchant for cheap liquor and big talk. Even so, her love for him had never wavered. If she loved him enough, she reasoned, she could change him.

Unfortunately, things hadn't worked out like she planned.

"How old was Adam when it happened?" Justine asked to turn her thoughts away from the scene playing out in her mind.

"He was in his twenties is what Coral Jo said. Said she read in the paper that he went out for a run and dropped dead one day of a heart problem." She snapped her fingers. "Just like that."

"That's awful. So young to go."

Abby frowned. "Life's like that," she said matter-of-factly. "My Joe wasn't thirty when the cancer took him." Again they fell silent. "You've got to tell him," she continued a few minutes later. "Even if you don't, he's bound to find out eventually."

Justine looked up sharply. "You wouldn't say anything, would you?"

"I didn't say I would or wouldn't. What I said is *you* should." Abby shifted the books to the crook of her arm and picked up the black bags at her feet. "It's the right thing to do."

The right thing to do was so far in the past that any action taken now would be too little too late. She shook her head. "I can't."

"Honey, you were just a kid back then, a scared kid with no options."

Options. Is that what it was called when a child gave birth to a child, then gave him to someone else to raise?

"I need to eat something," Abby remarked. "But I'm a mess. Want to meet me at the Dixie Café in a hour?"

Justine nodded absently, her mind still floating between what she should do and what she had done so long ago. Never, on close inspection, could she reconcile the two.

Abby frowned and whirled away in a cloud of dust. "About Luke Butler. Be careful, Justine. It's a small town," echoed down the narrow stairway. Her sister punctuated the warning with a sharp bang, the sound of the attic door closing a floor below.

Seconds later, a second door, the one to the outside, slammed, and Justine stood alone, alone with dangerous, traitorous thoughts of Luke Butler. A wisp of dark hair across a tanned forehead and the scent of Ivory soap on broad shoulders were the only memories she had allowed herself over the years since they had gone their separate ways. Now, in the attic of the old church building, with weak sunlight playing off sparkles of dust in the air, she fell headlong into the world that had once included Luke Butler.

"No," she said in a whisper that barely carried across the confines of the attic. "I can never tell Luke."

Justine slapped at the top of the box nearest to her. She dissolved into a cough, choking more on the name she had finally spoken than the dust that swirled around her.

"Tell Luke what?" The voice was deep, strong, and unmistakable.

Luke Butler was back.

two

"Justine Kane."

Luke's velvety soft southern drawl wrapped around her name and held it in a fluffy cloud of mixed memories. Unbidden, they began a parade before her eyes, bright snapshots of a world long ago and long forgotten.

A smiling sophomore nobody on the arm of the senior captain of the football team slid past, followed by the same pair on a sandy riverbank on an August night. Finally there came a lock of inky hair and a three-inch square of a baby blanket the color of a robin's egg. Justine's heart slammed against her ribs, and a single tear welled in the corner of her eye. She squeezed her fingers around the roll of packing tape in her hand and tried to think of something to say.

The shadowy figure eased into a shaft of daylight and leaned against a tall stack of boxes. "Cat got your tongue, Darlin'?"

Justine suppressed the urge to pinch herself as he came into focus. If Luke Butler wasn't real, so much the better. Unfortunately, from the top of his dark head to the tip of his dark brown hiking boots, he looked as real as the stack of boxes he leaned against.

The clothes he wore were casual, a mix of faded denim jeans and a neatly pressed blue oxford shirt. His hair was longer than she remembered and looked slightly unkempt, as if the soft dark waves grazing his freshly shaved jawbone had only recently been tossed by the morning breeze. A small cellular phone hung clipped to his belt, and a gold watch glittered against the dark tan of his wrist.

He still had the look of an athlete about him, with a breadth of shoulders and a bulk of chest that she did not remember there on the day he left Bailey's Fork. Of course, he hadn't been much more than a kid then, barely nineteen and full of rage. The Luke Butler who stood before her now was one hundred percent full-grown male.

Funny, he still had that look of anger about him.

Justine climbed to her feet and wiped at the dust she knew her jeans had attracted. It was a futile gesture at best, for a morning spent in close quarters with nearly a century of cobwebs and grime would never be cleaned away with a few swipes of her fingers.

Luke pushed away from the boxes and took a step forward. Somewhere beyond the musty scent of old hymnals, Justine caught the faint scent of Ivory soap.

She inhaled that scent and held it deep inside, deeper than the memories she'd tried to forget. "I wasn't expecting anyone up here," she stammered, then cringed at the inadequacy of the first words she'd spoken.

"Don't suppose you remember me." His drawl still apparent, the words stung rather than caressed.

Justine almost laughed out loud at the foolishness of his statement. Instead, she hid her face in the shadows.

"Luke Butler," he said with a dip of his head.

Sunlight teased the planes of his rugged face and illuminated eyes that were the deep blue-green of still water in an East Texas lake. Curling her fingers into tight fists, Justine expelled a quick breath.

"I know," she said. Painfully she groped for words while he measured her with a stare that held more than a little contempt. "I remember," she added when their gazes met.

"I wasn't sure you would."

For a moment, she thought she saw discomfort flash across the face that, as Abby had predicted, looked like it belonged on the big screen. His lips tilted slightly into a weak smile, and he shook his head.

"You're exactly like I remembered," he said.

Words evaded her, so she settled for watching sparks of filtered sunlight dance across the mess she'd made of the attic and herself. Instantly, she became the same nobody she'd been twenty years ago, the nobody to whom Luke Butler had mysteriously bestowed his precious attention. Even now, at the ripe old age of thirty-six, she felt the butterflies begin to rise in her stomach as the silence between them lengthened.

She said a silent prayer for guidance and another for strength. The packing tape she held in her hand fell off the tips of her fingers and rolled across the floor, landing inches away from the toe of Luke's boot.

"How've you been?" he finally asked, watching the tape spin to a stop.

"Fine," she answered in a voice several octaves higher than her own. "And you?"

"I'm good."

"Good." The smile she attempted cooperated. "So, what are you doing here? In the attic of the old church, I mean."

"I was downstairs." His gaze swung to her. "I heard a noise."

"Oh." She blinked away the memories those eyes still held and tried again to look like she'd forgotten all about them. About him.

"What're you doing here?"

Justine shrugged. "Cleaning."

"I see."

The air between them thickened. On the other side of

the red-and-white-checked curtain, a horn honked two floors below on First Street. Justine jumped, her heart racing. "So, you've done quite well for yourself," she said with what she hoped would be a casual toss of her head. "Football, right?"

"Yeah, for awhile." He looked amused for a moment, then something akin to sad. "Four years ago, I went into the broadcasters' booth." The words escaped in a low breath, followed by a soft, "I did all right." Defiance replaced his sadness and turned the angles of his face to stone.

"Did? As in past tense?" As soon as she'd asked the question, Justine wanted to reel it back in.

Luke rocked back on his heels and stuffed his fists into the pockets of his jeans. "Yeah. I'm retired."

"Must be nice," she said. The stupid grin began to waver, so she pursed her lips and gave it another try.

Luke stared directly into the beam of light, showing her a profile less rugged than she'd expected. His nose bore no signs of the rough way he'd made his living, and his chin still held the upturned brashness she remembered.

"Adam told me you'd gone off to school. Got a degree in psychology or something."

"Social work." She studied the floor a moment, then lifted her gaze to meet his. "I'm sorry about your brother." She paused. "I didn't know."

"I miss him. He was something special," Luke said, eyes shut.

An uncomfortable silence once again hung between them.

"Will you be in town long?" Justine finally asked, giving up on the false smile when she realized her innocent question sounded for all the world like a pickup line. Flames rising in her cheeks, she ducked her head and pressed the last hymnal into the box, then fumbled around for the tape to seal it.

"Haven't decided," he said in an offhanded manner as he leaned to retrieve the tape. "Why?"

"Well, I don't know. I'm sure you've got a lot of catching up to do."

His eyes narrowed. "You think so? Like what?"

She reached to accept the dusty tape roll, and their fingers brushed. It took all the control she had not to jump backward and make a total fool of herself. "I don't know. Catch up on old times. Visit the sites."

He shook his head. "Like the football field or the country club?" He paused. "Or maybe that little spot over by Lakeside?"

Justine froze, and her heart jumped into her throat. The lake had been their special place, a hideaway for two teenagers who never should have been alone. Thankfully, Luke's cellular phone rang, saving her from an answer. Not that she had one.

"Gotta go," he said when he hung up the phone.

"It was good to see you," she said with the last of her breath.

"Yeah." He turned and headed for the door, then stopped abruptly. "You're still living on Third Street," he said over his shoulder.

A statement, not a question, but still she felt she should answer, perhaps explain why at the age of thirty-six she still lived in her childhood home. "Yes, I—"

"I'll be by around six," he interrupted. "To catch up on old times."

"Six? I don't think—"

"Have plans?" He cast a dark glance over his shoulder.

"Plans? Well, no, but—"

"Good." His frame filled the doorway, then disappeared

into the darkness of the staircase. Unlike her sister's exit, Luke's heavy steps shook the very foundation on which she stood.

"Hey," she shouted. "I don't think this is such a—"

"Six," echoed across the rafters and settled in the pit of her stomach.

Justine bit her lip and tried not to cry.

❧

"You didn't cry, did you?" Abby asked, shoving the last of her cheeseburger with extra ketchup into her mouth.

"Cry?" Justine stabbed a French fry with her fork and held it up to the light. "Of course I did." She faked a smile. "When I got home and saw what a mess I was. Would you believe I had to wash my hair twice to get the cobwebs out? That's why I was late."

"I'm serious." Abby's eyes narrowed. "I couldn't believe he showed up not five minutes after I left and I missed it. You didn't let Luke Butler see you cry, did you?"

"Keep your voice down." She looked past Abby to the crowded room. "I'd rather keep this between us."

"It's a small town, Honey." Abby smiled a Cheshire cat smile. "Everyone's bound to know sooner or later."

"Not if you keep your voice down."

"Denial rears its ugly head again." She slapped at Justine's hand. "Like Dad used to say, put the fork away if you're not going to eat."

"Speaking of Dad," Justine said, "have I told you about my visit with him yesterday? He really looked good. I'm wondering if the new medicine's working."

With an efficient gesture, Abby emptied part of Justine's fries onto her plate and reached for the saltshaker. "I'm glad you had a nice visit with Dad, but what I really want to hear about is your visit with *him*."

"Him?" Of course she knew exactly who Abby meant, but teasing her bossy elder sister was too easy and too tempting. Besides, it took her mind off the calamity waiting to happen this evening.

She sighed. "Him. Luke. Your first conversation in, oh, twenty years. Did he act surprised to find his old flame is now a highly respected and still very single church secretary?"

Justine frowned and said nothing. Outside the window, the single stoplight in Bailey's Fork switched from green to yellow, then to red. She began to turn the remaining wilted fries into a rather interesting freeform sculpture.

"You didn't tell him anything about yourself, did you?" Abby licked a dab of ketchup off the corner of her mouth. "Well, of course you didn't."

"What do you mean by that?"

"He probably didn't ask." She shrugged. "Guess you were right. He's just here to do a little real estate business. It has nothing to do with you at all."

"Actually he wants to get together tonight." As soon as the words were out, Justine longed to retrieve them.

"I knew it!" Abby pounded her palm on the uneven table and set the water glasses dancing. "I just knew he was here to take up where he left off with you."

Justine leveled an impatient stare at her sister. "Abby, he said nothing of the kind."

"Oh, come on." Abby leaned closer and lowered her voice. "Why else would he want to see you?"

Why indeed? Justine pushed away the answers and reached for a cold French fry, then dropped it back on the plate. "It doesn't matter. I'm not going to see him."

"Yes, you are! You are definitely going to see him!"

"Hush!" Justine looked around to see if Abby's outburst had attracted any attention. Thankfully it hadn't. "I'm just not going to be home, plain and simple. Want to go to a movie?"

"No. I have four children, it's a school night, and yes, you will be home because you cannot hide from Luke Butler forever."

Leaning against the back of the red plastic seat, Justine folded both arms around a chest that ached with a pain twenty years in the making. A dark brown delivery truck slowed to a stop across the street at the bank, capturing her attention. Seconds later, a tall man in a dark uniform emerged, offering a fortuitous change in the conversation. "Say, isn't that Hank?"

"Hank who?" Abby asked, auburn eyebrows raised.

"You know who," Justine said. "Hank Hawthorn."

Abby shrugged. "So?"

"So didn't the same Hank Hawthorn sit next to you in the second pew last Sunday? And the Sunday before? And, if memory serves, the one before that?"

Abby's gaze darted to the window, then swung back in the direction of the center of the diner. "Where's our waitress? We're almost out of salt."

"Three weeks in a row at church, Abby, and that's a record. And is it true that he braved Tina's seventh grade band concert as well as one of Lainey's soccer games?"

"Yes," she said meekly. "Where *is* that waitress? I told Charlene never to hire college kids. They're never around when you need them."

Justine stifled a giggle. Seeing Abby on the receiving end of what she usually gave out was more than fun.

"Pastor told me Hank was going to be heading up our church's offering to the new 'Feed the Elderly' ministry," Justine said. "He volunteered one of his delivery trucks for the weekly run. Isn't that great?"

Abby frowned. "We're not talking about Hank and me. We're talking about you."

"What a nice guy," Justine said, hoping to keep the focus off her for as long as possible.

"Well, that's just it," Abby finally said. "He's always looking after everyone else."

"Including you and the kids," Justine reminded.

Abby nodded and stabbed a fry into the lake of ketchup flooding the center of her plate. "I know," she said slowly, obviously pretending to concentrate on the food in front of her. "But a man like that is bound to run out of steam eventually. Can you believe he wants to buy the old Lakeside Cabins campground and use it as a church retreat? I mean, really."

Just then, the man in question came bounding down the sidewalk and jumped into the Hawthorn Services delivery truck. A moment later, he drove off in a cloud of dust.

"Looks plenty energetic to me," Justine said, motioning for the waitress to bring the bill. "If you aren't interested, I just might be."

Abby's green eyes widened and jealousy mingled with shock. "Justine Kane! What in the world would you want with Hank? You tell everyone who will listen you're perfectly happy living alone."

Justine laughed. Abby was smitten, possibly more than she cared to admit. After all she'd been through, the time had come for her sister to start trusting again and let a man in her life once more. Justine decided to turn up the heat a little on her teasing, just to get Abby's attention.

"And I am happy, but I could use a guy like him." She paused for effect. "On church newsletter day, that is. Do you have any idea how hard it is to get those heavy boxes to the post office?"

Abby laughed, and Justine joined her.

"Seriously, Abby," Justine said, leaning closer to her sister to avoid the nosy ears of Miss Emma, the lead-footed librarian, and the seven other ladies of the Bailey's Fork Library society, who had just seated themselves en masse at the next table. "You care about him, don't you?"

Abby nodded again, and both of them waved to the library ladies. "Hank is great."

"Then what is it?" Justine traced the edge of her red-and-white napkin with her index finger and watched her sister squirm. "What's wrong this time?"

Over the years, Abby had become a master of ruining potentially great relationships. All it took was for the guy to be single, handsome, and gainfully employed, and she would find a reason to get rid of him. On the other hand, Justine preferred to watch the show from the sidelines. While she could see plainly what her sister needed in the way of a man, the right one for Justine had never come along.

Well, maybe once, but that was a long, long time ago. Before she began her walk with the Lord. That Justine Kane had been content with a man so far removed from God's Word he'd had a picture of the devil tattooed on his right biceps. For a brief moment, she wondered if it were still there.

Abby slid her a sideways glance and let out a long breath. "Don't you have to *be* somewhere?" she asked pointedly.

"Nope. The newsletters are safely at the post office and the rest of the afternoon is mine."

"Until six."

Justine breathed through the blinding shot of pain in her gut and somehow managed to keep from rising to bolt out of the restaurant. "Hank Hawthorn's a nice Christian guy and—"

"And he treats me good and loves my kids." Abby nodded. "Okay, I'll talk about Hank, but only if *you* talk about Mr. Wild Thing."

The standoff lasted exactly ten seconds. Justine knew because one of the library ladies had begun to count while the others scribbled furiously on notepads.

"Ten," came the shout from Miss Emma. "Now who managed more than five words from the phrase Bailey's Fork?" Emma asked.

"Fine," Justine said, shouting over the commotion. "But I'll warn you right now, there is nothing to tell." She paused to let the shrieks at the next booth die down. "You first," she finally said.

Abby nodded and bowed her head. "Okay, about Hank. I know all the good things about him, but. . ."

"But what?"

"But it's been so long since I depended on a man for anything. Lainey will be ten in a couple of weeks, and she never even met her poor daddy." Abby expelled a slow breath. "Maybe I need a little work in trusting the Lord and allowing Him to provide instead of always depending on myself."

"You think so?" Justine returned the smile.

Her sister's spine seemed to lengthen by several inches as Abby sat tall and squared her shoulders. "Oh, look who's talking."

"What do you mean?" Justine asked as another cheer went up from the library ladies' table.

"I mean, you just might need to actually turn a little over to Him on occasion too."

Having heard the accusation more than once from her big sister, Justine merely nodded. Getting in the backseat and letting the Lord take the wheel was a constant trial for her, to be sure. "I'm working on it," she answered truthfully. "Be still and know that He is the Lord, right?"

"Right." Abby pushed the plate away and leaned both elbows on the table, resting her chin in her palms. "So?"

"So what?"

"So tell me about Luke. Does he still look the same? Was that old spark still there?"

Justine shook her head. "It was dark and dusty, and if there were any sparks flying, they were hidden under layers of attic grime."

"Well, never mind," Abby said, eyes widening. She motioned to the window. "I can see for myself."

Justine followed her sister's gaze. Standing on the steps of the First National Bank of Bailey's Fork was the Wild Thing himself. Luke had obviously done a little cleaning up of his own in the hour and a half since their chance meeting. Gone were the jeans and oxford shirt, replaced by a crisp white dress shirt and a tailored suit in a deep blue-green that surely matched his eyes.

Engrossed in conversation with a man whose back was to the café, he failed to notice he had an audience. Justine studied him, then said a silent prayer for strength, understanding, and more than a little control.

Head bent, perhaps to catch the words of the shorter man, Luke began to nod. Sunlight played on hair so dark it looked almost blue.

Without warning, Luke looked over in the direction of the café. Justine quickly glanced away.

"Oh my," Miss Emma declared. "That Luke Butler has grown up to be a fine man. He always returned his books on time, you know."

A sharp pain radiated from Justine's elbow, and she looked down to see Abby hold her fork there, ready to jab her again. Without a word, her sister nodded toward the window.

Moving slower than she ever thought possible, Justine swung her gaze back in the direction of danger. *And lead me not into. . .* She blinked hard, then finally allowed her gaze to settle back on Luke. "Temptation," she said aloud.

"Indeed," Abby answered. "And there he is now."

Without so much as a smile or a wave, Luke held up both hands to reveal six fingers. Then he had the audacity to turn his back and walk away, leaving the little man to scamper after him.

three

Justine watched the red numbers on the clock by her bed change from four forty-one to four forty-two. Only the sound of her breath marred the silence of the room that was, on most occasions, her favorite place to be outside the Lord's house.

With the small raise she'd received from the church last fall, she'd purchased the most extravagantly romantic antique four-poster bed and pine dresser. The sale of her old and serviceable full-sized set netted just enough for a beautiful quilt in shades of rose and mint green and a set of shams and a dust ruffle in a lovely Battenberg lace.

The matching lace curtains rustled with the soft breeze, allowing the distant sounds of a child's laughter to float through the rose and ribbon pattern. The sweet giggle wound around the room to capture her heart.

It reminded her of the laughter, and the tears, of her own child. Her own child. She tested the weight of that thought and put a hand on her stomach. So long ago she had cursed that rounded stomach, blaming the child inside rather than herself for a life she knew would be ruined.

That had not happened. Quite the contrary. Once the secret of her shame was safely deposited three counties away, Justine stepped back into the life of a high school student as if nothing set her apart from the others. Only the small scar on her belly and the lock of dark hair safely hidden behind her newly earned driver's license hinted at the truth.

Silly, after all these years, she still carried that lock of hair in the same place. A lock of remembrance, she called it. A badge of shame, she'd always thought it to be.

Shame.

She swallowed hard and tried to push the word from her mind. Shame was the devil's work. Pastor said more than once, when you go to God and ask forgiveness, it is done. He has forgotten as soon as He has forgiven.

" 'As far as the east is from the west, so far has He removed his transgressions from us,' " she whispered, face turned to the breeze.

She knew the verse from Psalms all too well, and still the shame nagged at her. The clock downstairs chimed five times, reminding her of a more pressing concern.

Luke Butler was back.

In a town the size of Bailey's Fork, their paths would cross often. How would she manage it?

Justine took a deep breath, let it out slowly, and climbed to her feet. She walked the length of her bedroom, slowing only to search in vain out the window for the source of the ever-present laughter, until she knew she might wear a path in the deep beige carpet.

With a sigh, she landed on the bed with a most ungraceful flop. The pictures on the nightstand rattled and the crystal vase shook, spilling a drop of water onto the polished mahogany top. Rose petals from the vine that had climbed the back porch for half a century floated in a miniature harbor atop the dark surface.

Quickly she dabbed at the spot with the edge of the Battenberg sham, then replaced the pillow on the bed and snuggled into the soft covers. Facing the ceiling and her fears, Justine realized the truth could no longer be denied. She had a big problem, a problem that looked to stand about six-foot-one and weighed about a hundred and eighty pounds. A problem that went by the name of Luke Butler. What she didn't have was a solution.

"What would you have me do, Lord?" she whispered into the freshly washed pillowcase. "I am one of Your children now, and yet the sins of my past continue to haunt me." She waited in the stillness for an answer.

"Blessed are you who weep now, for you will laugh"—words from the book of Luke came to her.

"Did you have to pick Luke, God?" she asked with a wry smile as she sank deeper into the feather pillows and tried to calm herself by humming every hymn she could think of. An eternity later, out of song material, she rolled over and faced the clock.

Five-twenty. Outside the window, the childish laughter had disappeared, drowned out by the low rumble of an engine. A motorcycle engine.

Fear gripped her, and the breath that had come so easily moments before now stalled in her throat. Justine flew out of bed and ran to the window, throwing the lace panel aside in time to see Wilfred Plotz, her next-door neighbor, disappear behind the tall hedge of red-tipped photinas with a leaf blower. A leaf blower that sounded a whole lot like a motorcycle.

Her breath discharged in one long rush of air, and her spine straightened. She snapped the curtain into place and smoothed back the hair that had fallen into her eyes.

"This is silly," she said as she checked her image in the dresser mirror. "He is just a man, and he probably just wants to buy my house." She smiled. "Of course," she said as she turned toward the door. "Silly."

He'd already bought an old abandoned church building, the First National Bank, and if the talk around town was true, he'd made an offer for the Dixie Café, the old First Street Bakery, and the empty country club building. A place to live among the kingdom he had amassed seemed a logical next step. What better place to pick for purchase than the home of the one man who hadn't bought into the glory and hype surrounding the now famous Luke Butler?

Her father hadn't cared that Luke was captain of the football team, nor did he seem impressed that he had set state records in several categories. All he cared about was that the daughter he loved ran wild and Luke Butler ran with her. That was enough to make Arthur Kane refuse to allow the boy in his house and later refuse to allow him in his daughter's life.

The leaf blower roared to life again, and this time Justine barely jumped. Instead, she shook her head and smiled a wry smile.

"This time I have options," she whispered. "I am a grown woman. I will not be a prisoner in my own home." She raced down the stairs and snagged her purse. "If Abby won't go to the movies with me, I'll go alone."

❧

The one night she decided to go to the movies alone, there was nothing she wanted to see. On any other night, she would have found something; but tonight, of course, the only two offerings at the Bailey's Fork Cinema were a blood-and-guts action movie and a children's cartoon featuring various characters from a galaxy known as Garks-burg. As neither of these choices appealed, Justine drove around the block and contemplated her next move.

The clock on her car dash read a quarter to six as she turned right on First Street and drove past the shuttered windows of the empty church building. In stark contrast, the Dixie Café next door held quite a crowd, no doubt the remains of the Tuesday night bridge group that met above the photography studio two blocks away.

Justine stopped at the light in front of the café and turned up the radio. A fast-paced praise song ended and another slower one began. Her gaze drifted to the right and to the steps where she had seen Luke standing with the stranger. The same steps where he'd looked across First Street to hold up six fingers as a reminder of their meeting.

The memory of the grim defiance on his face startled her once more, almost as much as the horn honking behind her. Justine pressed the gas and blinked hard to dispel the image.

Turning left, she came to a stop at the corner of Elm and Second and waited while a group of seniors crossed the road and loaded into a church van. These were her people, their trip tonight a product of the sole senior citizens' program the city fathers of Bailey's Fork had seen fit to fund.

Next year, maybe she could stir the collective consciences of city and county officials and add another day to her pet project. For now, she could take comfort in the fact that with the Lord's help and Hank Hawthorn's delivery truck, these sweet folks would have a weekly meal in addition to their weekly outing. If only there were a place where the less fortunate of them could go. A place where people like her father would find more than three meals a day and adequate but sterile care. She shook away the thought and forced a smile in the direction of the seniors.

Quite a few of them waved, all having known Justine practically since birth, and she returned the gesture, one eye on the car clock. When the way had cleared and the last gray-haired matron had boarded the bus, Justine continued down Elm at a slow speed.

The houses were older here, unlike the much newer

neighborhood where Abby had moved several years ago, but Justine loved them all. Her favorite, the home where she grew up, sat a block away on the corner of Third and Maple. A turn to the right and she would be only a few feet from the driveway.

She checked the clock once more. It read five fifty-four.

Leaning forward as far as she could, Justine looked down Third to see if she could tell whether Luke had arrived at the house. Unfortunately, the Plotzes' photina hedge prevented her from having a clear view. She grasped the wheel and leaned a notch farther to try for a better look.

When her horn honked, she jumped and let her foot off the brake. The car shot forward, careened off the road, and bounced onto the curb. Justine jerked the steering wheel to the left in order to miss the bright red farm-style mailbox looming inches away and plowed directly into one of Bob Biggsworth's real estate signs.

The car ground to a halt, throwing Justine against her seat belt full force. The air bag inflated a millisecond later, enveloping her in a cloud of white. She batted at the fabric and pushed her way toward daylight until finally she managed to tame the safety device.

Shaking hands reached for the door handle only to find she couldn't have held it if she tried. Justine blew out a long breath and leaned back against the seat, closing her eyes.

"Get it together, Justine," she said under her breath. "You're fine, and the car can be repaired. Just breathe."

"I don't think she's breathing," came a distinctly masculine voice.

Justine's eyes flew open to find Luke Butler and two of her neighbors only inches from her nose. Luke had opened the door, and his hand rested on the slightly bent steering wheel. He still wore the business suit she'd seen him in earlier in the afternoon. Her sudden movement sent Mr. and Mrs. Plotz scurrying backward, but Luke didn't flinch.

One dark brow rose slightly when she did not respond. "Cat got your tongue?" he asked in his silky drawl.

"Is she breathing, Luke?" Mildred asked. "Because I saw a special on TV about head injuries, and if she's got one of them, she might quit breathing at any minute. You better check to see."

Luke cast a glance over his shoulder at Mildred, then looked back in Justine's direction, scorching a path from her eyes to her chin and back again. With his free hand, he loosened a burgundy tie covered with small medallions of navy and gold.

"She looks fine to me, Mildred. Color's good, and there's no bruises that I can see," Wilfred Plotz said from his vantage point on the sidewalk.

"You sound like you're judging tomatoes at the county fair," Mildred said. "What do you think, Luke? How does she look to you?"

"Now how's he going to know how she looks, Mildred?" Mr. Plotz protested. "Every day since the girl was born we've seen her. Thirty-six years I've been Justine's neighbor. If anyone should know, it would be me."

"Oh, that's ridiculous," Mildred said.

The pair stepped away and began to argue in earnest. Through it all, Luke maintained his steady gaze, although the hand grasping the steering wheel had begun to turn white at the knuckles. Her gaze drifted from his large hands to the gold cuff links on his white dress shirt.

"You still breathing, Darlin'?" he finally asked.

Before she could gather a clear picture of him once more and manage more than a weak nod, a police cruiser pulled up alongside the car. Justine stifled a groan.

The occupant, Eli Watts, Bailey's Fork's lone officer on duty on the evening shift, had been a former teammate of Luke's at Bailey's Fork High and an usher at church. Their rivalry on the field was legendary, and even now they seemed to circle each other like alley cats looking for a fight.

"Well, well, Lucas, my friend," Eli said as he clasped hands with Luke. "Long time, no see. I heard the NFL finally got tired of you, but I never expected to see you back here." Luke muttered something in return, which Eli seemed to ignore. "Hey, Justine," he said as he turned to her, "you didn't mean to do that, did you?"

Justine shook her head, then instantly regretted the action when stars appeared in her line of vision. *Another male, another stupid question,* she wanted to say.

"It was," she actually said, speaking slowly as her thoughts scattered, then gathered again. "An accident," she finished.

"I saw it all," Mildred Plotz said, her voice jumping an octave in excitement. "She come to a stop right there, then leaned over the wheel real far. Looked like she was spying on somebody."

Justine groaned again.

"Then she honked her own horn," Mildred continued.

"How'd you do that, Justine?" Eli asked.

"With her. . . ," Mildred began, then looked down at Justine's chest, suddenly at a loss for words.

"Well, alrighty then," he said, studying the points of his alligator skin cowboy boots as a fine blush colored his cheeks. "I guess I've got enough to file a report. Good thing the sign stopped you or your car would have landed on the front porch."

She looked past the dangling "Sold" sign to see the

front porch of the former residence of the late Ella Hawthorn less than five feet away. *Thank You, Jesus*, she prayed silently. *I could have gone to glory on this one*. From the book of John, words poured forth, although she could not be sure if she said them aloud or just heard them in her mind.

"From the fullness of His grace we have all received one blessing after another."

That she hadn't rammed her car into the house and been seriously, possibly fatally, injured was definitely a blessing, although she had her doubts about the crowd assembled around her now. That could have easily been called a curse.

"You need an ambulance or anything, Justine?" Eli asked as part of the sign gave way and landed in the middle of her hood with a loud bang. The noise resonated in her skull, and she jumped. A shaft of pain shot up her chest and settled between her eyes.

"Justine?" Eli asked again. "How 'bout I call the boys over at the hospital and just let 'em have a look at you? Wouldn't hurt."

"No," she said in a hoarse whisper. "Don't."

Her head ached and no doubt a bruise would show where the seat belt had held her, but considering what could have happened had Bob's real estate sign not been in her path, she felt just dandy. She'd feel even better if she could go home and hide.

Justine fumbled with the seat belt, then gave up when her hand became hopelessly entangled with the remnants of the air bag. Without breaking eye contact, Luke managed to release the belt and clear the safety device out of the way. The fading rays of the evening sun danced across his hair and highlighted the deep bronze angles of his face.

He'd shaved since their last meeting, and Justine felt the

insane urge to touch his cheek to see if it was as soft as it looked. Her fingers twitched and moved, then fell back in her lap.

"Now don't move her, Luke," Mildred warned. "I saw this episode of—"

"Will you hush, Mildred? What do you want him to do, leave her in the car in the middle of his front yard?" Mr. Plotz shouted, and the war between them spurred on again.

Justine swiveled in the seat and placed both feet on the ground. Her head began to throb in earnest, and every muscle in her body screamed in protest. Luke offered a hand, which she refused.

"I'm fine, really I am," she managed through a clenched jaw as she climbed out of the car and straightened to a standing position. That position lasted just long enough for her to meet Luke's stare again.

Then she teetered forward. Luke stepped in to steady her with a tight grip on her forearm. When her legs refused to budge and her arms did not move to her command, Luke took over.

The world tilted when he swung her into his arms and set off in the general direction of her house.

"Easy there," she heard Eli say.

"Watch out for that brain injury. She just might have one," Mildred called.

"Shut up, Mildred," Mr. Plotz retorted.

"Still doing okay?" Luke asked without meeting her confused stare.

"I'm fine," she repeated, whispering to quiet the hammers banging inside her skull. "The back door's almost always unlocked. If you could just let me down I'll—oh!"

Luke bundled her closer and took the old wooden porch steps two at a time, slowing only to throw open the back door. "Typical small town," he said gruffly.

Marching through the kitchen and down the hall to the front parlor, he deposited her on the sofa. The impact of landing on the cushions jarred her. She bit her lip, more out of surprise than pain, as Luke stepped back and appraised her with a solemn stare.

"You got a brain injury?" he asked, not a hint of humor in his voice as he began to pace between the fireplace and the front window.

"No!" she shouted, then held her head against the explosion the single word had caused.

"You're just fine then?" he asked. "In spite of the fact that you almost took off my front porch."

"Your front porch?"

She tried to sort out the meaning of his words, but when Luke stopped pacing and leaned against the fireplace, and any hope of concentration faded. He stood close, too close, to the one thing in the room she did not want him to see, the small framed snapshot of a dark-haired infant.

His gaze followed hers and fixed on the picture. Picking it up off the mantel, he weighed the silver frame in his hand and studied the baby. As he leaned over the picture, a lock of hair fell into his eyes. So close was his concentration, he seemed not to notice.

Time stood still, and only by the sheer strength of will did Justine continue to breathe. *Lord, give me the words to tell him,* she prayed. *Abide with me and let me rest in Your strength.*

In the twilight, Luke's eyes glittered, and his thick lashes cast a shadow across high cheekbones. He palmed the tiny photo and gave her a slow, searing look.

"You and I have a lot to talk about," he said, pointing the picture of their baby boy straight at her heart.

four

She looked like a cornered rabbit. And why shouldn't she? After all, he *hadn't* exactly been Mr. Congeniality in their previous two encounters, and he *had* just pulled her out of a wrecked car. Luke concentrated on slowing his racing heart and tried to ignore his racing mind. Maybe he should just back off and try to have this conversation another time.

A deep intake of breath brought the spicy sweet scent of apple pie, taking him back to the days of his youth when food had been scarce and the football coach, bless his soul, always had a sack lunch waiting in his locker before the big Friday night games. Always, in the bottom of the bag, there had been a thick slice of pie.

As he contemplated this, his gaze traveled from the lace curtains on the wide windows to the grandfather clock in the corner and finally to Justine, the one bit of unfinished business still left in his life. She sat perched on the edge of a fluffy-looking white sofa filled with fluffy-looking white lace pillows, a woman ready to run if he'd ever seen one.

A quick glance over his shoulder told him the fancy leaded glass front door had been bolted and chained, leaving her only one exit. To prevent her quick escape, he shifted positions and blocked the path between her and the still open back door. Any question about postponing the conversation evaporated as the old feelings washed over him in waves.

Twenty years ago he'd been a cocky kid with a burning hunger in his gut that surpassed the actual hunger he felt on a daily basis. Son of a father who died young and a mother who cooked and cleaned for others to make ends meet, he never quite made it into the country club set that people like the Kanes ran with.

Even when football elevated him to a position of honor, he could never escape the stigma. Oh, he was good enough to cheer for on Friday nights, as long as he didn't show up on their doorsteps on Saturday to date their daughters.

The irony of it all was that the country club he once stood on the edge of, a kid peering through the fence at a life he could never be a part of, was now another property on his vast list of holdings. Wouldn't those who scorned him be surprised when they found out his plans for that place?

"Thank you," Justine whispered, cutting a soft path through the hard edges of his attitude. "For helping me to get home, I mean."

She looked up at him through eyes threatening tears and his knees almost gave way. Her hair, still as blond as he remembered, had been twisted into a braid and spilled over the shoulder of her navy blazer, reaching almost to the waist of her fashionably faded jeans.

Of all the ways he'd imagined her in the last twenty years, poised, graceful, and well, serene, had not been one of them. The pretty girl he remembered had become a beautiful woman. This complicated everything.

As if she'd noticed him staring, she flipped the braid over her shoulder and crossed her legs to reveal a pair of conservative loafers. The model of suburban domesticity, Luke could easily picture her at the wheel of a minivan with a couple of kids and a dog.

His kids.

His dog.

The thought both intrigued and terrified him, and he

shook off both feelings with a roll of his shoulders. With a casualness he did not feel, Luke leaned against the fireplace mantel, glanced at the climbing pink roses out the window, then gave her a quick nod.

"You're welcome," he finally managed, even though his gut felt like he'd been hit by a speeding freight train and his throat felt like someone had stuffed it with cotton.

He continued to contemplate the roses as they swayed in the soft evening breeze. Twenty years ago, he had picked a hand full of them for Justine on their last night together. Did she even remember? Probably not.

A woman with her looks had probably received her share of bouquets, all of them no doubt much more impressive than the pitiful offering he had made. The sad little blooms and the broken branches most likely never saw the inside of Justine's fine house.

The grandfather clock chimed the quarter hour and Justine jumped. "I suppose you're wondering why I was two blocks away when I should have been here waiting for you," she said when the last ring had stopped.

Her statement, made so innocently, almost made him laugh. "Not really," he said slowly, swallowing the cotton along with the bile that had begun a slow climb. "I might have spent most of my life as a jock, but I'm not *that* dumb."

Of course he knew why she was two blocks away. She never intended to meet him. Not that he'd given her a chance to object.

Justine had the decency to color a soft scarlet before she turned her head. Grabbing a fluffy pillow, she hugged it to her chest, and for one brief moment, Luke remembered what it had felt like to be in her arms.

He pushed away the thought with a shake of his head. "Look, maybe we should do this another time."

"Maybe we should." She touched her forehead and winced.

"You're hurt." He leaned closer and examined the blue smudge that darkened her skin just above her left eye. "You got an ice pack?"

"It's just a little bump." Pushing the pillow away, her gaze fell to the picture in his hand. She opened her mouth to speak, then clamped it shut, her face suddenly pale.

"Cute kid," he commented for lack of something meaningful to say.

"May I have it please?" she asked in a trembling voice, rising to reach her hand toward his.

He gave the picture one last look, noted the tiny face with the shock of dark hair, then handed it to her, being careful not to allow their fingers to touch. Eyes downcast, Justine stuffed the frame into the pocket of her blazer and shrunk back in silence. The braid fell forward, and it took all of Luke's strength not to reach out and touch the silky rope. His fingers curled around that thought until he shook them and released the image.

"I'll get the ice," he said quickly.

This time she didn't protest, so he headed for the kitchen, a room he'd barely noticed on his first trip through. The minute his boots left the hardwood and hit the tile floor, he stopped. Even in the semidarkness, he could tell that unlike the other room, this one had not changed a bit.

Luke hit the switch, and the room blazed with the light of an ancient hanging lamp in the form of copper-colored grapes and leaves. He blinked hard and let out the breath he hadn't realized he'd been holding.

"There's a small towel on the table," Justine called. "You could wrap a few ice cubes in it, I guess."

"Yeah."

The wooden table still stood in the center of the room, a huge round oasis of oak in a sea of white tiles and even whiter cabinets. On its scarred surface, a bowl of green apples and a newspaper were the only signs that someone lived there. Other than that, the place looked as if it rarely saw much use.

So Justine wasn't much of a homebody. He stalked across the floor and grabbed the towel.

A glance to the right and he could see the chair where old man Kane used to sit and read his paper, all the while watching what went on between him and his precious Justine on the back porch. Wadding the towel between his fingers, he called up the image of the old man.

Dismissing the logic that told him Arthur Kane had to be old enough to be retired by now, Luke pictured him as he had been the last time their paths had crossed. Studying the face of his nemesis, he called to mind the full mouth that never had a good thing to say to him and the wide-set blue eyes that said volumes on their own.

His left hand balled into a fist. He pulled back and aimed his fist at an imaginary image of a frowning old man Kane, then froze when a pair of abrupt and uncomfortable realizations came to him.

Strange, but those same heartless features, the cold blue eyes and the cruel mouth, formed into a rare and wonderful beauty on Justine. Stranger still, the man he always thought of as old couldn't have been much older than Luke was now.

What would he have done if some kid with a devil tattooed on his arm came chasing after a daughter of his? The answer pained him too much, so he pushed it away.

"How's your father these days?" he asked casually as he twisted the length of terry cloth, then rubbed it over his arm where the scar still remained from the removal of the awful tattoo.

"As well as can be," he heard her say.

Mixed emotions shot at him from all angles. On the one hand, news of the old man's good health should have made him happy. The better to exact his revenge. On the other hand. . .

He retrieved the dishtowel and stalked to the ancient Kelvinator, opening the door to find two cartons of yogurt, a six-pack of diet soda, and an empty container of milk.

"Looks like you need to make a grocery run, Justine, Darlin'," he said under his breath as he opened the freezer compartment and fished around for a few pieces of ice in the bin.

The pickings were slim here too, he noticed. Nothing but a couple of frozen dinners and a carton of coffee ice cream broke the expanse of iced-over space. Above the fridge, he found the source of the apple pie scent, a fat red candle with a label proclaiming its scent to be fresh cinnamon apple tart.

"You know this really isn't necessary. I can manage just fine." She sounded nervous.

"Hey, I'm pretty good with an ice pack. Got my medical training in the NFL. Just don't ask me to operate."

Luke cringed at the poor attempt at humor. Jamming three ice cubes into the towel, he slammed the refrigerator door and left the kitchen and its ghosts behind.

"Here you go." He knelt to press the towel to her forehead. "You need anything else? Something for the pain maybe?"

Her fingers curled over his, and the wide blue eyes barely blinked. Fear. He'd spent too many years in the NFL not to know fear when he saw it.

"I'm fine, really," she whispered.

"So you said." He kept his voice low as well, mesmerized by the pale slender fingers entwined in his. A lifetime ago, those hands held his and swore to never let him go. How easy that promise had been to break.

The moment, had it happened in another time and place, might have been a tender one. His gaze shifted from her fingers to her lips.

"Justine, you in here?" Eli Watts called from the back door. "Anybody home?"

Luke rose at the sound of the deputy's voice, and Justine jumped to her feet as well. Reaching to turn on the lamp beside her, she dropped the towel, and ice slid across the floor in three directions. Luke put the pieces back together and handed them to Justine along with the towel. When he looked back at Eli, the man wore an amused expression.

"Well, hello, you two," he said, removing his white Stetson as he sauntered into the room.

Short dark hair spiked in all directions, and his khaki uniform wore spots of mud across the front. The light caught his silver star and bounced toward them across the dark planks of the floor. A competition born on the high school playing field flared anew, and Luke squared his shoulders as if to take the man head-on.

Eli broke into a broad grin and swiped at his brow with the back of his free hand. "Administering a little first aid, were you, Lucas, old buddy?"

"You could say that," Luke snapped. "She's got a nasty bruise over her right eye." He turned to look down at Justine. "You really ought to have him call an EMT to look at it."

"It's a wonder a bruise is all she's got considering how close she came to running up on the porch over at the

Hawthorn place." Eli smiled at Justine, and Luke fought the urge to wipe the grin off his face. "You sure you don't want me to call someone?"

"No, I am fine." Her shoulders sagged. "But my car. How bad is it?"

"Don't you worry about your car." Eli flashed her a look that made Luke's fists curl. "I took care of it for you."

There were laws against hitting a deputy, weren't there? At that moment, Luke hardly cared.

Eli shook his head. "Looks like all you got was a dent in the hood. Zeke's gonna haul it down to the garage and see what he can do. Zeke's my older brother," he added for Luke's benefit.

"I remember," he said, jaw clenched. How could he forget the largest defensive lineman ever to play for Bailey's Fork High? For that matter, Eli's exploits on the playing field had nearly eclipsed his own. Strange, Eli had ended up back in little Bailey's Fork rather than opting for making football his livelihood too.

Eli's radio squawked to life, and he reached for it. "I'll be right there," he said when the noise stopped.

Justine reached for Eli and grasped his hand to shake it. "Thank you, Eli," she said. "Tell your brother I'll call him in the morning."

"I'll do that." He replaced the Stetson. "The law calls," he said and turned to retrace his steps out the back door. "You two behave," he shot back over his shoulder as his boots thudded on the wooden steps outside.

"I should go too," Luke said. "And let you take care of that bump."

Justine touched her forehead but said nothing. Her lips softened to almost a smile. Outside the window, the rosebush scratched against the screen.

With each scratch of the thorns came the reminder of why he had returned to Bailey's Fork. Of what he had to do.

The grandfather clock ticked off several seconds before Luke found his voice. "Take care of yourself."

Finally she looked away. "I will."

He brushed past her to make a quick escape.

"Luke?"

Her soft and somewhat shaken voice brought him to a dead stop on the threshold of the back door. Slowly he turned to see her standing just inside the kitchen. Long rays of late afternoon sunlight cast an orange glow in the room and bathed her in a warm light.

From where he stood, she looked like a frail angel come to earth. His memories, however, told him otherwise.

"Yeah?" he answered, probably a little too gruffly.

She slipped a hand in her jacket pocket. "Did you buy the Hawthorn place?"

He nodded.

"So," she said slowly, looking none too pleased. "It looks like we're going to be neighbors."

"Yeah."

He inhaled another deep breath of apple pie–scented air and watched her struggle with the silence between them. Once again he felt the overwhelming urge to run, to get out of that house and as far away from Justine Kane as his legs would take him.

Sadly, he knew that nowhere on earth was far enough. He'd spent twenty years trying to do just that and had failed miserably.

Maybe he should have considered spending another twenty more doing the same thing before he attempted this again. Rethinking the whole situation suddenly had a good sound to it.

In the meantime, he would just have to lay low and try to avoid any contact with Justine Kane. Not that it would be easy since he'd bought a house less than two blocks away.

One last breath of apple pie and another glance at those blue eyes and he bolted out the open back door. He'd made it halfway home before he realized he hadn't even said good-bye.

five

He hadn't even said good-bye. In fact, Luke Butler seemed to have dismissed her entirely. Justine smiled despite his snub. Maybe Abby was wrong about him. Maybe her worst fears of Luke Butler being a constant reminder of the past and a presence in her future were unfounded after all. Maybe his appearance in Bailey's Fork would have no effect on her at all.

"And maybe pigs will fly," she said under her breath as she crossed the kitchen floor to stand at the back door.

Of course his presence would affect her. To think otherwise was ridiculous. For twenty years she'd managed to hide her mistake behind a veil of impeccable behavior. Now that Luke had returned, she had to face the fact that the biggest mistake she'd made had been to walk away from her responsibilities without any consideration for the other two people involved. She stared at the wide shoulders and broad back of the man crossing her lawn and tried in vain to ignore the gravity of the situation. The secret she'd kept for so long would soon come out. It had all but happened already.

Resolutely, she squared her shoulders and turned away. With a heavy heart, she expelled a long breath and scanned the room. The crumpled dishcloth lay in the sink where she'd left it, and the newspaper still cluttered the table. Beyond the door, the silver frame once more held its place on the corner of the mantel.

Everything seemed the same, and yet everything had

changed. Luke Butler had bought a house practically in her backyard. She would see him on the street, at Bailey's Fork's only grocery store, and maybe even at church on Sunday. How would she handle it?

Justine tugged at the end of her braid and reached to switch off the light. "There is nothing to handle," she whispered as she slipped off her loafers and left them at the bottom of the stairs. "I am just a brief moment from his past. Probably the last thing on his mind."

Stifling a yawn, she cast a quick glance at the photograph on the mantel. Only Abby, her father, and her pastor knew the child in the picture was her son, Brian. How would she admit to Luke and eventually to the citizens of Bailey's Fork that the morally-upright church secretary who volunteered with seniors every Monday had given birth to a child at the age of sixteen, then blithely returned to become valedictorian of Bailey's Fork High and president of the honor society?

Worst of all, how would the information affect her position at church and her standing in the community? How would she ever lobby to get the senior center built when her reputation stood in tatters?

Justine shook her head and lifted her eyes to heaven. "Forgive my pride, Lord," she whispered. "Just as You forgave my sins."

Holding on to that thought, she went through her regular nighttime routine. Only after she had applied lotion, combed out her braid, and slipped beneath the covers did she glance at the clock.

"Seven-thirty-three?" Justine sat up and plumped the pillows behind her. Her shoulder throbbed, so she shifted into a more comfortable position and smoothed the quilt in her lap. "Now what?" she wondered, then spied the mystery novel she'd begun two nights ago.

Three pages and fifteen minutes later, she gave up trying to concentrate on the gently nosy elderly lady and her current predicament and gave in to what concerned her most. Her son had a father, and that father had come back to Bailey's Fork. What could she do? What should she do?

So far the Lord had been silent on those questions. Her thoughts swung from Luke to the frightened girl she had been all those years ago and the decision that had been made for her. She'd made her peace with God and with Brian, the dark-haired boy who'd blessedly found her, but she'd never made peace with herself. Could it be because she hadn't made peace with Luke Butler?

"What do I do now, Lord?" she asked again. "How do I undo the mess I've tangled myself into?"

How indeed? The perfect life she had created in Bailey's Fork hid an ugly truth. Justine Kane might be a church secretary with high standards and higher morals, but she was human. And that human had made a horrible mistake one summer night on the banks of the river, a mistake she had come to love. A mistake that she had to admit to Luke. And to Brian.

Tucking the novel under her Bible on the nightstand, she folded her hands in her lap and closed her eyes. Offering up a prayer for guidance, she opened her eyes, picked up the phone, and dialed.

As it rang, she said another quick prayer, this time for confidence. "Brian," she said when the young man answered. "It's Justine. Are you busy?"

"Hey, Mom. What's up?"

Justine smiled at the sound of his deep, smooth voice and at the relatively new experience of a nearly grown man calling her Mom. "I like it when you call me that," she said. "But you don't have to, you know."

She heard his sigh and pictured his blue-green eyes and the dark lashes that fringed them. Without warning, those features shifted and blurred, reforming in the image of Luke Butler.

"I thought we cleared all this up. I want to, okay? Why else would I spend the bulk of my freshman year chasing leads on you instead of chasing University of Houston coeds?"

"Because you have a perfectly nice girlfriend." She paused, picturing the sweet fair-haired girl Brian had introduced as his Becky. "And you have a wonderful, understanding mother and father who raised you. Never forget that," she added.

Justine gave silent thanks for the couple who had loved and nurtured her precious son. Their sudden death in the first months of Brian's college career had prompted his search for his birth mother.

"If I ever did, you would remind me." He laughed. "I'm beginning to believe Becky, the future psychologist, when she says I get my stubbornness from a family member. I wanted you in my life, and I plan to call you Mom, and that's that."

"Okay," she said with a chuckle. "I get it."

The next few minutes were filled with Brian's updates on his grades, his latest job delivering pizza, and the upcoming summer session at college. Finally, when her son ran out of things to say, Justine cleared her throat and plunged into the subject that was the reason for her call.

"Brian, we need to talk."

"Sounds ominous." His laugh this time held little of the humor that the last one had.

Ominous, maybe. Life changing, definitely, for both of them.

"What's wrong?"

Justine shifted positions again to ease the pain in her shoulder where the seat belt had left its mark. "I'd rather not go into it on the phone. What's your schedule like this weekend?"

"All clear," he said.

The clock downstairs struck eight. "Can you come here or should I come to Houston?"

"I'll be there." He paused. "Are you sure you're all right?"

"I'm fine." She gripped the phone. "I just want you to meet someone."

"Sounds mysterious."

A few minutes later, despite Brian's persistent questions, she ended the call without giving up any more information.

"Well, it's done, Lord," she whispered as she replaced the receiver on the cradle. "I hope I'm doing the right thing."

Sliding out from under the covers, she padded to the closet and exchanged her sleep shirt and heavy socks for a pair of jeans and a plain navy T-shirt. She ran a brush through her hair and headed downstairs. On her way to the back door, she slipped into her loafers and pocketed the spare key from its hiding place beneath the basket of rose petal potpourri on the sideboard.

Before she had time to reconsider her mission, Justine found herself at Luke's front gate. She pressed open the filigreed iron gate and stepped inside, pausing to admire the quirky home, one of her favorites on this street. The warm night air blew softly, carrying with it the sweet scent of magnolias from the tree next door.

Only the distant sound of a dog's bark and the soft rustling of leaves disturbed the small-town silence. Overhead the first stars shone as only they can in the country, but the bright white moon shone through a wisp of clouds, a definite portent of rain ahead.

Justine inhaled the familiar scent, closed the gate as silently as she could, and began the short walk to the front porch of the old Hawthorn house. Like icing on a wedding cake, the place looked as if it had been carved from sugar icing by a baker gone mad. Row upon row of lacy trim fought for attention among the various porches and balconies of the two-story structure. Lights shone through lace curtains in two of the downstairs windows and cast a pattern of shadows on the gray-painted porch boards. In the center of it all, beside a double door of deep mahogany and leaded glass, hung a pair of brass lantern-style lamps that provided enough illumination to light the entire front porch as well as the yard beyond.

Her gaze swept over the well-kept lawn and stalled at the two ugly ruts where her car had dug into the freshly mowed grass. Bob Biggsworth's sign had been removed, and a fresh mound of dirt stood in its place, no doubt to cover the evidence of her accident. Tomorrow she would have to make arrangements to pay for the damages to the lawn. Tonight, however, she had to attend to damage control of another kind.

Bolstering her courage by reciting the Twenty-third Psalm under her breath, Justine reached a hand to ring the bell, then jumped back when it opened immediately and Luke stepped into the light. He had changed into jeans and a denim shirt left open to reveal a white T-shirt beneath it. His dark hair glistened with dampness as if he'd just stepped out of the shower, and his feet were bare. Behind him, light bounced across the polished hardwood floor and revealed a stack of moving cartons and a large wardrobe box that had been partly opened. She'd obviously caught him in the middle of unpacking. Instantly her courage dwindled to nothing, and her feet itched to run.

"I wondered how long you were going to stand on my porch."

A devastating smile punctuated Luke's slow-as-molasses Texas drawl. When she didn't respond, he raised one dark brow in a questioning slant.

"What's the matter, Darlin'? Cat got your tongue?"

Frozen, Justine's lips tried to form an answer, something that would allow her to gracefully remove herself from the situation and the porch. Before she could manage it, Luke stepped inside and gestured for her to follow.

"No!" The volume of her answer shocked her, and it stopped Luke in his tracks. He turned to give her a curious look.

"I'd, um, rather sit out here if it's all the same to you," she said, gesturing toward the swing hung at the far end of the porch.

"Sure," he said slowly.

"Thank you."

He gave her a sideways glance as he shut the front door and followed her. "Are you all right?" he asked when she'd settled onto the swing and he'd taken his place in the porch rocker across from her.

She nodded and dug her nails into her palms as her eyes avoided his by studying the porch boards and counting the nails that held them together. An eternity later, she managed to meet his questioning stare.

He'd made himself comfortable, long legs stretched in front of him and crossed at the ankles just inches from the toes of her shoes. "You look beautiful," he said.

Luke leaned forward and rested both hands on his knee.

The scent of Ivory soap teased her nose as the wind rustled the leaves of the magnolias. A lacy pattern of light and dark spilled through the curtains and played across the angles of his face.

"I like your hair loose," he said, his voice as low as the breeze. He paused to assume a more casual position, and the ancient rocker creaked in protest. "I always did."

Trembling, she slipped off her loafers and tucked her bare feet beneath her. The swing chains rattled, distracting her until their shaking stopped. The quaking of her insides continued, however, and she wrapped her arms around her midsection to no avail.

"How's your head?" he asked softly.

"Fine," came out in a rusty croak. "I'm sorry about your yard. I'll pay for the damages."

"That's not necessary," he said. "As long as you're not hurt, it's all right."

"I insist," she said, brushing a strand of hair from her eyes.

"Just try." He grinned. "Maybe I'll let you cook dinner."

She giggled despite the knot in her stomach. "Given my cooking abilities, I'd advise you to take the money."

Luke shifted positions and regarded her with a slow, appraising glance. "Eli Watts hasn't changed much since high school."

Justine looked up sharply, confused at the sudden shift in topic. "I suppose not," she said. "I don't see him much. Thank goodness," she added. "I mean, I don't make it a habit to. . .oh, you know what I mean."

"Yeah." His eyes sparkled in the porch lights. "I think I do."

They shared a smile, then allowed an uncomfortable silence to fall between them. A horn honked over on First

Street. "I forgot how quiet this town is," Luke said. "It's nothing like Houston."

She knew he had played some of his football career in Houston, but until that moment, she hadn't given any thought to the idea that he and his son had lived in the same city. Had their paths crossed? In a city the size of Houston, the possibility was unlikely. Still, like most Texas boys, Brian had declared himself to be a huge football fan. Had he without knowing attended his father's games and cheered for the man who had given him life?

Swallowing the lump in her throat, she inhaled a deep draft of magnolia- and Ivory soap–scented air and found her voice. "I have something to tell you."

He gave her a swift smile followed by a dubious expression. "Oh yeah? Sounds ominous."

six

"Ominous," Justine repeated. "That's the second time I've heard that word tonight." She took a deep breath and let it out slowly. With effort, she met his surprised stare. "I don't know where to start."

"The beginning seems to be the obvious place." He sounded annoyed, or perhaps curious. In either case, he seemed anxious as well.

"All right," she said slowly. "The beginning it is."

Luke nodded and sat back, crossing his legs at the ankles once more. Justine said a prayer for strength and forged on. "What do you remember about us, Luke?"

"I remember too much, Justine," he said in a husky whisper. "What's your point?"

"My point," she continued, "is that when you left, it wasn't completely over between us."

He held up a hand in protest. "Hold on, Darlin'. When I left, it was because it *was* over between us. You said as much on your daddy's back porch."

"I know, but. . ."

"But what?" His voice had risen, and his casual demeanor was gone.

"But I didn't know I was. . ." Again she paused, at a loss for words.

A slow smile spread across his face, followed by a nod of his head. His eyes narrowed with what looked like contempt. Justine's heart pounded with the realization that he must have guessed her secret.

"I think I know what you're getting at here, Justine," he said slowly. "It's about us. Then and now. What we had, and what we could have again. Right?" He leaned forward, a predatory animal on the verge of a strike. On his face he wore a satisfied look. "You saw what you missed out on and want another chance."

Confused, she opened her mouth to protest. He closed it with a rough and unyielding kiss that slid her off the swing and halfway into his lap.

Justine recoiled in horror and spilled out of his arms and onto the porch floor. Swift jabs of pain radiated up her arm and into her sore shoulder as she half-crawled and half-ran to escape the man she thought she knew.

When he caught her by the arm and swung her around to face him, Justine let out a strangled cry as a sickening wave of anger mixed with the terror welling up inside her. Luke released his grip and stared at her in stunned silence.

"Never touch me again," she ground out as she gulped furiously for air.

He held his hands out to her as if he were surprised. "But I thought this was about us."

She took another step back and wrapped her arms around her sweatshirt. Forcing a calm expression to her face, she looked beyond where he stood to watch the thick green magnolia leaves sway in the breeze.

"Oh, I get it." His voice was cold and harsh. "No matter how rich and famous I am, I'm still not good enough for a Kane."

"That's not true." She dared a look in his direction, then blanched at his angry stare. "Please just listen. This is important." Justine squared her shoulders and forced back the urge to panic. "I'd like you to meet someone," she said slowly, fighting to keep her voice even and strong. "It's important."

"Go home, Justine," Luke said as he stormed past her to disappear inside and slam the door.

❧

Exhausted from lack of rest, the last person Justine wanted to talk to at work Friday morning was her sister. As usual, Abby's call had come at exactly the wrong time, but putting her off did no good. When Abby couldn't get her on the phone, she often marched in to speak to her in person.

"Let me get this straight," Abby said. "You drove your car into Ella Hawthorn's house, and Luke Butler carried you home? Literally?"

Justine touched the bruise on her forehead with her fingertip and tried to ignore the curious look from the other occupants of her office. Thank goodness her sister hadn't heard about what happened after that.

"I'm working, Abby." She offered the young couple in front of her a quick smile. "I'm going to have to call you back." She hung up quickly as her boss, Pastor Dan Mills, arrived and handed her a thick sheaf of papers.

"Trouble?" Dan asked, giving her a cursory examination with brown eyes that glittered beneath iron gray bushy brows.

"No more than usual." She transferred the papers he'd given her to a file folder and reached inside her desk for a pen. "How did the city council meeting go?"

"It went well." The pastor fished a pair of gold-rimmed reading glasses out of his blue striped shirt pocket and set them on his patrician nose. "I see you've recovered. From the accident, I mean."

Heat flamed her cheeks, and her gaze fell to the floor, where she studied the gray and white pattern on the tiles. "So you heard."

He chuckled. "Bailey's Fork is a small town, Justine,

and it's not every day that the church secretary mows down one of Bob Biggsworth's real estate signs." His thick iron-colored brows gathered in concern. "Are you sure you're all right? I heard over at the café this morning that you had to be carried home after they got you out of the car. Then the mayor told me that Luke—"

"Yes, I'm fine," Justine remarked as she handed him another set of files and stood to reach into the filing cabinet for extra folders. "Don't these people have lives?" she muttered under her breath as she closed the cabinet door and turned to see the pastor still watching her intently.

"I've upset you," he said. "I'm sorry."

"No, really, it's fine. I shouldn't be surprised that the return of the prodigal would be cause for comment. Oh, the Chancellors are here to see you," she said with a nod over her shoulder.

His gaze locked with the young couple at the door, and a smile emerged. Subtly, Dan leaned toward Justine and raised a brow, a long-standing cue between them to silently let her know he had no idea who they were.

"New parishioners," she whispered in answer to his silent question. "I told them you had a few minutes to spare before the mystery meeting."

Eleven-thirty on Thursday had been blocked out on his calendar for over a month, the note written in the pastor's own hand. When asked, he'd been uncharacteristically vague about the whole thing.

"An exciting proposition," he'd commented once. "Quite a wonderful opportunity," he'd said on another occasion. Other than that, he'd kept mum about whatever he planned to do for the two hours he'd blocked out of what was normally quite a busy day.

He checked his watch. "I'd like you to sit in on the next

meeting, Justine. There are some exciting things about to happen within our church and within the community, and I'd like you to be an integral part." He paused. "If you're interested."

"Of course," she said. "Do I get one last hint?"

He shook his head. "No hints, but I will tell you that God is truly working in mysterious ways this time."

"Mysterious, eh?" She chuckled. "Now you've really got me curious."

Dan laughed. "Order in chicken dinners for three from the Dixie Café, and plan on taking lots of notes."

He turned to exchange a warm greeting with the couple waiting, and Justine sighed. After last night, a new and exciting project just might be more than she needed to take on right now. Brian would arrive sometime tomorrow with the expectation that he would meet someone important. How in the world could she pull this one off? After last night, Luke certainly wouldn't be talked into stopping by for a visit.

"Justine?"

"Yes," she replied, dragging her thoughts away from her dilemma.

"You might want to call your sister back while you have a chance," Dan said over his shoulder, punctuating the jest with a wink.

She called the café, then tried Abby, luckily speaking to her answering machine instead. Half an hour later, the Chancellors emerged from the office. Pastor saw them to the door, then returned.

"I see my appointment has not arrived yet, so why don't you grab a pen and paper and come into my office. I'll fill you in on the basics of what's going on."

She followed him into the office and waited while he

took a seat at the neatly organized desk. A pair of blue upholstered chairs had been pulled up near the edge of the desk, and she sat in the one nearest the wall.

Dan removed his glasses, folding them into his shirt pocket. "As you know, Justine, we've been cooperating with several area churches to develop a program for the seniors in our area. You've had a large part in coordinating that effort, which is why I want to include you in this."

Justine thought about the roadblock caused by the ladies boarding the bus behind the Dixie Café last evening and nodded. "They're provided transportation and a meal on a weekly basis. The three churches in the area take turns hosting."

"That's right," Pastor said. "But this only takes care of their needs once a week, which isn't nearly enough for some of these folks."

Justine nodded. After her mother's death, her father had left his architecture firm to become a champion of the cause of the elderly. When he could no longer carry the torch due to the encroachment of his illness, Justine took over and had used her connections within the church to help the elderly community in any way she could.

"What we really need is a program that could be implemented on a daily basis." She sighed. "But that's impossible given our limited funds. And the city council just won't listen."

He leveled a solemn look her way, and for a moment, she felt like a child caught misbehaving in church. She tugged at the green silk of her skirt and forced herself not to panic.

"I understand your frustration and applaud your efforts," he said, hands folded in front of him. He took a deep breath and let it out slowly. "If Bailey's Fork could fund a program of this magnitude without going through those bureaucrats in the city council, would you consider heading it?"

Justine's jaw dropped. "Me?"

Pastor Mills nodded. "I've spoken to the other church and community leaders, and they all agree that, given your talents and your degree in social work, you're the best candidate for the job."

"Job?"

Her heart raced as she contemplated all the good that could be done with a project that would reach all those in need. What an amazingly wonderful way to honor the Lord and help the dear elderly folks of Bailey's Fork.

"But I have a job," she said slowly.

"Your leaving would most certainly be our loss, although I assure you that we will still see one another at board meetings and on Sundays." He smiled. "I have it on good authority, though, that you just might know someone who would like to take over the office."

"I do?"

"Your sister, perhaps?"

"Abby?" Her sister had complained about her job checking at the grocery store for years. She complained of sore feet and aching muscles and especially of a rigid employer who frowned on absences caused by the raising of four children.

"Do you have another sister?" He shrugged. "Unless you can't give her a recommendation. In that case, we would definitely have to list the opening in the paper and take our chances."

"Oh no, of course I can recommend her," she said quickly. "She's very bossy. She'd be a great secretary for you."

He chuckled. "Then it's settled."

"What would this job entail?"

"At first it would be mostly paperwork, I'm afraid," he said slowly. "Applying for matching grants, securing permits, and the like. But once we get our building renovated—"

"Building? You mean there will be a real center for seniors?"

The pastor nodded. "The plans are for a multipurpose facility with the ability to provide meals as well as recreation and even some long-term care for those who need it." He paused. "Like your father."

Justine's mind raced with the possibilities her new position might offer, until reality brought her joy to a crashing end. "There has never been enough funds to even consider expanding the program for one extra day, much less considering anything of a larger scope. How are we going to do this?"

"It looks like there may be an answer." The pastor smiled as his eyes looked past her to the open door. "And here he is right now."

"He?" Justine asked, thoroughly confused.

Dan rose and extended his hand. "Justine, I understand you've already met our generous benefactor."

"I'm sorry I'm late," the all-too-familiar voice said in a slow-as-molasses drawl.

Justine swiveled in her chair, and her gaze collided with the cold stare of Luke Butler.

"Welcome, Luke. Please, come in."

Luke didn't move, nor did he acknowledge her presence.

"You know," she said as casually as she could, "I'd better go see what's taking the café so long to bring lunch." She stood poised to leave, but Luke's presence in the door prevented her escape.

"So, Luke, word around town is you saved my secretary's life." The pastor gave him an expectant look. "Sure would have hated to lose good help."

"I hardly think that's what happened," Justine said quickly. "Now if you two will excuse me."

Luke didn't comment. Nor did he move out of the way.

Dan cleared his throat and sank into his chair. "Yes, well, I suppose even though the two of you are previously acquainted—"

Luke snorted in disgust.

"As I said," the pastor continued. "For the purposes of the minutes of this meeting—which you should be taking, Justine—I should make the formal introductions then."

Justine ignored the barb and scanned the small space between Luke and the outer office, wondering if she could move fast enough to escape.

The pastor cleared his throat. "Luke Butler, say hello to Justine Kane, the director of your project."

"Director?" His voice laden with venom, he raked her with a stony expression, then turned to face the pastor. "You've got to be kidding."

seven

"Actually, I'm quite serious," Dan said. "Won't you have a seat? If you have reservations about Justine's ability to handle this job, I can assure you her qualifications are extensive."

Justine pointed her note pad at Luke. "I'm just as surprised as you are."

"I find that hard to believe," he said under his breath.

How in the world would he get out of this one? If things were to go as planned, Justine could not be a part of this project.

Luke scanned the neat cubicle Pastor Dan Mills called an office while he worked on an appropriate story. His focus fell on Justine once more and stalled there. Legs crossed at the ankles, she looked every bit the part of a church secretary in this proper pastor's office. He knew better, though.

The nerve of her acting so proper when she'd come on to him last night, then backed out at the last minute. *What do you remember about us, Luke?* she'd asked in her sweet-as-silk voice. What didn't he remember? He stifled a groan.

"Luke?" The pastor's voice broke through the beginning of a favorite memory, the one involving a hot summer night and an itchy wool blanket by the banks of the lake.

"Yes?" he answered with difficulty.

Dan straightened his spine, and his face lost all its warmth. His bushy caterpillar-like gray brows gathered in the center above eyes narrowed to slits. In all his dealings with the pastor, he'd never seen this side of the man.

"Unless you can give me a specific reason, I'm going to have to insist our church's involvement in the project is conditional upon Miss Kane's being the director."

So the two of them were in collusion on this. No church support without Miss Perfect's participation. At least Justine had the decency to look doubtful.

Luke's heart began to race. *Focus*, he told himself. *Breathe*. The room began to swim, but he refused to show weakness by sinking into the chair, even though his knees threatened to do it for him.

Focus.

Breathe.

The words became an all too familiar mantra, a comforting chant bridging the gap between his brain and his defective heart. Was this how it had been with his brother before he died? How much longer would he have to put up with the symptoms before the disease his father had bequeathed upon him claimed his life too?

With effort, Luke brought his thoughts and his body under control in a few seconds' time, although it seemed like an eternity. The averted attack left him shaky, but the situation forced him to act otherwise. He squared his shoulders and refused to wince at the residual pain there.

"Look, Dan, it's not Miss Kane's qualifications I have reservations about," he somehow managed to say. He leaned against the door's frame and acted like it did not hold him up.

"Oh?" The pastor frowned and gestured toward the empty chair, a blue upholstered monstrosity that had seen better days. "Sit down, Luke. I'd like to hear your concerns."

"You know, I don't think I will sit, Dan. And I don't think

there's anything to talk about."

He yanked the Harley keys out of his pocket and palmed them. At this point, his only plan would be to escape to fight another day, although his means of exit would most likely not be the motorcycle, at least not right away. Still, the bravado of flashing the keys to a big, loud, black macho machine seemed far superior to the threat of taking a long walk and a whole lot of deep breaths.

The preacher cleared his throat. "This project is for the benefit of the elderly citizens of Bailey's Fork and for the glorification of our Savior Jesus Christ. Now, you have raised a concern and it behooves us to discuss it, but I feel it only fair to warn you—"

"No, Dan, let me warn you. Unless you find someone else to head this project, you can count me and my money out."

Luke turned and walked out on the good pastor and his secretary. Justine stepped in front of him just inches from the exit, and had he not developed a keen ability to maneuver on the football field, he would have slammed directly into her. With fire in her eyes, Justine aimed her steno pad at him and hit him square in the chest. He barely felt it, although he certainly felt the close proximity of its owner.

"What do you think you're doing?" he asked, stunned more by her fury than her pitiful attempt to impede his progress.

"I think I'm getting your attention."

He chuckled. "Darlin' you've been doing that ever since you were fifteen years old and never once did you have to try this hard."

With that, Luke brushed past her and walked out into the sunshine. Donning his favorite leave-me-alone shades, he crossed First Street, stepped between a mail truck and a vintage Volkswagen of questionable color, and headed for the black Harley parked in the small lot beside the Dixie Café. Maybe by the time he put the key in the ignition, he'd feel strong enough to drive it.

To his right, the single light flashed from yellow to red despite there being no cars in sight to stop. He should have felt a wave of nostalgia walking across this street. After all, one of his many homes had been right there on First Street. A two-room, third-floor walk-up over the bakery, the sad little apartment had a hot plate and a bath down the hall shared by three other tenants and the day workers from the bakery.

Luke smiled despite the painful memory. At least he'd eaten well during those months. He cast a quick glance in the direction of the bakery, a red brick building now serving as the home of Biggsworth Real Estate and the law offices of Brinkman, Bailey, and Fawne. All these years later, Luke could still smell the sweet scent of cinnamon raisin bread baking.

"Hold it right there, Pal," Justine said.

The conviction in her voice shocked him into a quick halt. He turned to face the little woman with the big attitude.

"I quit," she said, and the color in her cheeks deepened.

"You quit?" He fought a laugh. "Quit what, Darlin'? You never had the job in the first place."

She took a deep breath and shook her head as she let it out. Right there in the middle of the sidewalk, he had the strongest urge to release her golden hair and watch the sunlight dance on the tips of the strands like it used to when they were kids. His fingers itched with the effort of restraint, and he jammed them into the front pockets of his jeans to keep him out of trouble.

Raising her chin in defiance, she aimed a blue-eyed

stare right at his heart. "Look, what's important is that we get this senior center built."

"I'm listening," he said slowly.

Justine looked past him. "If working with me is a problem, then, like I said, I quit."

She quit? The Justine Kane he knew had never quit anything in her life.

Except him.

He gave her a swift appraisal and took note of the professional-looking green silk skirt and prissy green blouse tied high at the neck, then slid his gaze a little slower down her long legs to end in disappointment at a plain pair of tan sensible shoes. Probably had a big purse full of junk to match those shoes, he decided. Most women who bought those kinds of shoes usually did.

Her demeanor, the prim and proper woman, stood in direct contrast to the Justine Kane he knew. She'd been something in those days, a little gal with a big attitude and a bigger love of life and all things pleasant and beautiful.

He'd seen glimpses of that Justine yesterday, but today she'd hidden them well. "You look like a church secretary," he commented.

"I am a church secretary."

Her stance told him she'd most likely swat him again if he said one more wrong thing, but the threat only served to amuse him. And after all he'd seen and done, it took a lot to amuse him.

"How did that happen? The church secretary gig, I mean."

"I found the Lord, and the job found me." She waved at someone behind him, then turned her attention back to him. "The point is, the older folks in this town have nowhere to go and often not enough to eat. They need a facility like this. I've prayed about it for years, and so have a lot of others."

Her sincerity amused him, almost as much as her speech about the Lord. The Justine he knew could never have become a preachy little church secretary. This had to be about the money.

His money.

"Back when I knew you, you swore you were getting out of Bailey's Fork as soon as you could," he said. "What changed?"

"Me." She bit her lip. "Everything, but I really don't want to discuss any of this right now."

He raised an eyebrow and looked down his nose at her. Someone on First Street honked and called his name, but he ignored them. The world telescoped into a place where he and Justine were the only inhabitants.

"That's not what you said last night," he commented as he reached to help a young mother having difficulty maneuvering a stroller onto the curb with a wailing baby.

His good deed done, Luke turned back to Justine with a smile. Rather than be impressed with his Boy Scout moment, she still looked as angry as ever.

"Where were we?" He ignored her frown. "Oh yes, we were discussing what you wanted to talk about last night."

"It's true you and I need to have a conversation, but tomorrow, not right now."

"Why put off until tomorrow what you can do today?"

She gripped her steno pad to her chest like armor and shook her head. "Right now what I want to talk about is the senior center. Are you backing out or not?"

If she ever looked more adorable, he couldn't remember when, preachy little secretary or not. Even though the woman had all but given him an engraved invitation to kiss her, then complained when he did, he couldn't hold it against her. Something about Justine Kane stirred his blood; it always had.

Every man had an Achilles heel, and Justine Kane was his. Of course, he never intended to let her know.

"Now that's a good question, Darlin'," he said slowly.

Justine always did like his smile, so he gave her his best television smirk and removed his shades. Turning on the charm, he narrowed his eyes and put on his best "I-am-incredibly-interested-in-you" look. The last time he attempted it, he ended up with a long-term contract on the Sports Network and a female television producer whom he thought would never stop calling him.

"How about you and I discuss it over lunch?" Without letting his smile dim, he calmly nodded toward the single eating establishment in Bailey's Fork. "Maybe you can talk me into it."

"Into what?"

She looked a little confused and a lot angry. Could it be his plan to impress her had missed its mark?

"Into whatever you have in mind," he said, easing his words out like syrup on a warm day.

Justine blinked hard, hooding her baby blues with a fringe of thick lashes. "You disgust me," she said in a voice that quaked with anger. To add insult to injury, she repeated the phrase twice, each time with increasing volume.

"What? What did I say?" he asked as he attempted to assess the situation.

Two blocks away, the lady with the stroller turned to stare. A couple of folks eating over at the Dixie Café cast a startled glance in his direction, too. Obviously the prim little church secretary's mouth was bigger than the baby's and louder than the constant din inside the café.

"Calm down, Justine," he said softly. "The whole town's watching you make a fool out of yourself."

"What did you say?" she ground out.

The cutest tinge of pink crept above the high collar of her church-secretary blouse and began the upward climb toward her lightly freckled cheeks. Luke ignored his urge to smile and concentrated on being charming.

"You know, Darlin', maybe we ought to go back to my place and talk about—"

"You are unbelievable." She paused, fuming. "I cannot believe I actually thought you were going to do something good with all that money you've been flaunting." Her voice trembled again, and she made a wide slash through the air with her steno pad. "This conversation is over. You can do whatever you want with your money!"

"Oh really?" He lowered the wattage on his smile and watched while the pink in her cheeks turned crimson.

"Yes, really!" With that, she had the nerve to turn around and walk away. As fetching as she looked crossing First Street, he just couldn't let her get away with it.

eight

"Hold it right there, Justine!"

Justine whirled around in time to see Luke charging in her direction across First Street. Big and menacing, he wore anger not only on his face but also in his stride and in the air around him. Only her sense of outrage at the man's antiquated way of thinking kept her feet glued to the ground beneath the town's only working stoplight.

"I told you our conversation is finished."

"Not yet," Luke said. "Not until we settle this."

Gulping down equal doses of anger and apprehension, she fisted her free hand. She looked both ways to make sure First Street was empty of cars, then turned her gaze back to Luke.

"You made it abundantly clear you don't want me to work on your project, Luke, and I made it abundantly clear my Christian beliefs don't allow me to tell you what I think of your opinion."

He had the nerve to laugh, not just a chuckle but a deep, booming belly laugh, loud enough to shake the rafters in the old church building across the street. Something in the laugh rang hollow to Justine, as if he wanted her to believe he found amusement in something devoid of humor.

His laughter faded and dissolved. Still, behind the gleam in his eyes, Justine sensed a fine thread of hostility, possibly more.

"Actually," he said slowly. "I think disgusting covered it pretty well."

Justine fought the urge to cringe. She had said that, hadn't she? What sort of test had the Lord in mind when He allowed Luke Butler back into her life? Whatever it was, she'd done a lousy job so far.

Above her head, the light changed from green to yellow and finally to red. She contemplated her words and chose them carefully. "I shouldn't have said that," she admitted. "Please forgive me."

At first Luke didn't react. Finally, he cleared his throat and shook his head. "So you don't think I'm disgusting?" He squared his shoulders and seemed to grow a foot, so threatening was his posture. "C'mon, Justine, admit it. Your old man did."

He glared down at her, and those blue-green eyes seemed to slip beneath her skin to glide past her heart and into her soul. How dare he bring her dear father into this, especially when the man could no longer defend himself?

"As far as I am concerned, we're done." She glared back—or at least she hoped she did. Maybe if she held her pose long enough, he would get on the motorcycle he rode in on and ride out again.

Then she remembered Brian and her promise to him. Only for her son, and for what she realized was a wrong she had to make right, did she manage to say anything more.

"There is another matter I will discuss with you," she said slowly, looking past Luke to the big window of the Dixie Café, where several familiar faces stared in their direction. No doubt she and Luke Butler were fast becoming the talk of the town.

One of the familiar faces, she realized, was Eli Watts; he waved, but she ignored him.

"Why all the mystery, Justine?" Luke said as he turned

his gaze back to her. "I'm not real fond of playing games unless it's football."

He paused and let his gaze scorch a slow path from her head to her toes, then reverse directions to make a slow climb upward. When he met her stare again, he almost smiled.

Almost, but not quite.

"And you don't look like you're dressed for football," he drawled. "But with those shoes you just might beat me in a footrace."

His face softened slightly with the poor attempt at a joke, but the anger remained swirling around him in great stormy gusts. Justine searched her mind for an appropriate response and found it blank.

Luke shook his head. "Look, I'm the one who should apologize."

His sudden change of attitude confused her. "Apologize? For what?"

"For what I said about the project. To you and to Dan Mills." He crossed both arms over his chest and stared past her. "Maybe I overreacted. You were the last person I expected to see as a director of anything."

She stuck out her chin in defiance. "Because I'm a woman?"

"Because you're Justine Kane." Their eyes collided. "And I never figured you for a crusader."

"What does that mean?"

"A do-gooder. You know, someone who worries about old people and lost puppies. You always seemed to worry about. . ." He paused to smile. "Other things," he finished.

Her anger flared. How dare he make character decisions about her? He knew absolutely nothing about her life after the tenth grade.

He sighed. "I just keep disgusting you, don't I?"

"Maybe."

He gave her a sideways glance. "In any case, we still have the question of whether or not you intend to make good on your threat to quit."

"I don't remember phrasing my intention as a question."

Luke shrugged. "I told you I might be persuaded to change my mind."

"And I told you—"

He held up both hands, palms up. "I know, I'm disgusting. On occasion anyway." He paused. "But I've got a pretty good head for business, and I'm not going to pass on the best project director for the job, man or woman."

"But you said—"

"I know what I said. You surprised me, that's all." He frowned. "How about we get the details taken care of over lunch?" He cast a glance over his left shoulder at the Dixie Café.

"I don't think so. I'd rather settle this—"

"Best restaurant in town right over there, and there's never any wait for a table," he said, quoting verbatim from the sign that had hung beneath the café's green striped awning since 1962. His gaze locked with Eli's, and both men offered a curt nod at the same time. "Besides, it's the only restaurant in town."

Justine opened her mouth to respond, then felt the world tilt as a loud noise, the roar of an ancient engine and the squeal of tires, skirted her right ear. When the world righted again, she stood on the curb in front of the old church building, and Luke's hand held her elbow like a vise.

"What did you do that for?" she asked as she pulled away from Luke.

Luke gestured toward the retreating taillights of the

antique red-and-white Ford Fairlane belonging to Miss Emma. "Library emergency, I guess."

Justine shook her head. "It must be noon."

"One of these days the old gal's gonna come barreling around the corner and hurt somebody," Eli Watts called from the opposite sidewalk.

He'd forgotten to remove the red-checked napkin from his collar, making him look less like a lawman than ever. Ignoring Luke, he smiled at Justine.

"You all right, Justine?"

"I'm fine, Eli."

She straightened her blouse and tried to pretend her elbow hadn't begun to throb. Spending time with Luke seemed to be a dangerous pastime.

"Let me finish my chili, and I'll pay our speed demon a visit down at the library," he said as he hiked up his tan trousers.

"No, please, don't. She's been flying through here every day at noon since we were in grade school." Justine smoothed her skirt and stared past Eli to the diner. "It was my fault for standing in the road."

"Yeah, we was wondering about that," Eli said, removing the napkin, "why you were standing in the road, I mean."

Justine didn't have to question who else was wondering. In a small town, any business was everyone's business. "We were talking business," she said as several other diners joined him on the sidewalk.

Eli nodded and repeated her claim to the newcomers. In turn, they nodded as well. A few of them added their responses, although she couldn't make out the words over the sound of her heart beating in her ears.

"We hadn't thought of that," Eli finally said. "We was figuring you and Lucas here was busy renewing old acquaintances and that's why you was standing in the middle of the road and didn't see old Emma flying by."

Luke stiffened, and a muscle clenched in his jaw. The anger around him became a surging storm as the crowd in front of the Dixie Café continued to grow.

From where she stood, Justine could see the mayor, her hairdresser, three ladies from the church choir, and her English teacher from the sixth grade mingling on the curb. Several others were hidden in the deep shade of the awning, but she could have sworn she heard her dear neighbor Mildred Plotz say something about a head injury.

"Don't you have some crimes to solve, Eli?" Luke ground out.

"Hey, Luke," the mayor called. "How's our newest citizen?"

"Can't complain." He gave Justine a look that said just the opposite before turning to stare at the politician. "We still on for this afternoon, Sir?"

"Yessir. Two o'clock in my office, just like we planned." The mayor puffed his chest and smiled. "Channel 46 out of Houston's going to film the whole thing."

Luke shook his head and muttered something under his breath. "Now, Mayor," he said slowly, when he'd taken a breath or two, "I thought this was just going to be between me and you and the superintendent."

"My boy, when a citizen of our fair city gives such a momentous gift to the school district as the deed to the old country club, I feel the whole world ought to know." He searched the faces of those gathered around him, and they nodded in agreement. "If only your high school football coach was here to see the facility you named in his honor." He paused and looked at Luke with concern. "I hope I haven't overstepped my bounds on this."

"You bought the old country club?" Justine asked, incredulously.

He gave her a wry smile. "It was the only way I could get in."

Justine shook her head. "And how long were you going to keep this a secret?"

"I would have said something eventually," he said with a shrug. "At the right time."

While Luke carried on a perfunctory conversation with the mayor, Justine digested the information and took a moment to calm herself. By the time the man had finished speaking, she'd almost managed the task.

Then Luke turned around and everything went spiraling out of control again. She paused and said a quick prayer for her feelings to get out of the way and allow the right words to come. At least it seemed as though the crowd had begun to lose interest.

"Luke, it's time I told you something." She took a deep breath and plunged forward. "There's a young man I'd like you to meet. A special young man."

Justine gulped down a deep draft of air. She'd said too much, far more than she'd intended. Braving a look, she searched his face. Surely he knew now.

A look of understanding came over his face, and it was all she could do not to burst into tears. All the years she'd carried her secret, only to have it exposed on First Street for the world to see.

"A young man?" he asked, brows drawn.

Some of the color had gone out of his tanned skin, leaving white creases at the corners of his mouth. Numb, she stared at those creases, then slid her glance down to his neck and the open collar of his shirt. A vein on the side of his neck throbbed, the only sign of life she saw.

"Yes. His name is Brian." Again she paused to collect her thoughts. "Could you come over for lunch with us tomorrow around noon?"

"Brian."

The sound of Luke Butler saying their son's name was almost more than she could bear. How many times had she imagined him holding their child, calling his name, and loving him?

And loving her?

"How young?" Sarcasm laced the question.

"Young?" was all she could manage as the picture of father and son faded, and Luke slid into focus once more. Shouldn't he know?

He nodded. "Let me get this straight. You find me disgusting, and yet you intend to show me off?"

Confusion snaked into her consciousness. "Show you off? What are you talking about?"

"Famous football star returns. His old girlfriend can't wait to impress *Brian* with a meeting with the big star. Now you are the one who disgusts me, Justine." He turned his broad back to her and started across First Street. "And that, Darlin', is hard to do, because I've just about seen it all," he tossed over his shoulder.

"You idiot! Brian is not my—"

Luke whirled around. The world telescoped to a small expanse of First Street between the curb and the streetlight, and it contained only her and Luke.

With a predatory smile, he held up a hand to silence her. "You know, you always were a wild one. Once I figured out how to get through that icy exterior of yours, that is."

Anger blinded her as blood rushed to her temples to beat a rhythm in her ears. "You don't understand."

"Oh, I understand." He held his arms out by his side.

"What *you* don't understand is I'm not going to help you impress your boyfriend."

"Would you just listen a minute?" she shouted.

Without a word, he turned his back again and began to walk away.

"Brian is not my boyfriend! He's twenty years old, he's perfect in every way, and he is your *son!*"

Too late, she saw the crowd outside the Dixie Café had swelled rather than dispersed and every last one of them had heard her declaration. The film crew from Channel 42 in Houston, who were filming some background shots to go with the story on Luke Butler's triumphant return to Bailey's Fork for the evening news, heard it as well.

nine

Luke drew a ragged breath. As time and place telescoped to form a tunnel between him and the spot where Justine stood, he forced himself to exhale. For a moment, the intake and release of breath occupied him far more than the life swirling around him.

He stared at Justine, forcing himself to notice everything about her rather than to think of everything she'd just said. In the rush of the crowd, her hair had loosened, but it still could have used his hand to muss it up and release it from the granny-style hairdo. Her blouse looked disheveled as though she had dressed hurriedly, and her face had paled to an unnatural color.

"Luke, I. . ." Her voice disappeared into the roar of the blood in his temples and the noise of the crowd.

"Luke, I can't believe. . ." The mayor's voice rose above the din and fell again. Sounds and people pressed toward him in waves and someone turned a spotlight in his direction.

Think of her. Think of anything but what she said. As hard as he tried, the scattered images in his mind kept coming together to form one word, one idea, and one accusation.

Father.

The idea began to take hold, and it scared the life out of him.

Someone stuck a camera in his face, but he gently elbowed it away. Another clapped a hand on his shoulder, and he shrugged it off. Many offered congratulations or shared a laugh at the great joke of it all.

Father.

He held the word in his head and slowly allowed it to seep into his heart. How could he be a father? Testing the sound of it in his throat, he attempted to bring it forth.

"Father."

The mere speaking of the word drew the life right out of him, and were it not for the circumstances, he might have fallen to his knees. Somehow, he held his ground, squared his shoulders, and pressed through the mass of lights and confusion to reach Justine.

No words passed between them when their fingers touched, nor could he have answered if she had spoken. Using his slightly rusty football skills, he linked arms with her and pressed through the chaos with her in tow.

"Do you have a comment, Mr. Butler?" someone shouted.

"What do you have to say, Miss Kane?" came from another, someone she obviously recognized by the look on her face.

"Luke, our meeting," the mayor declared. "What shall I tell the press?"

Turning slowly with Justine still in his grip, Luke took a deep breath and forced his racing heart to slow enough to reply. The mayor stood no more than a foot away, and his ever-present smile had been reduced to a desperate frown. An expectant hush fell over those assembled, broken only by the insistent barking of a dog tied to a tree in front of the bank.

He met the fascinated stares of the men and women who used to watch him on the high school football field and probably continued to watch him on television. Finally, he swung his gaze and his attention to the pompous fool who used to be the principal at Bailey's Fork High School and was now the mayor. As principal, he'd taken great pride in singing Luke's praises to the press after every Friday night football game. In private, the same man had refused to allow his own son to associate with him.

How had he managed to be so civil with the pompous fool so far? *Because he gave me the respect I never had in this town. The respect I'm due. The respect my money and my fame has bought and paid for.*

Somehow none of it mattered at this moment.

"The press, Son, what should I say?"

Son. Luke shot past the idea of his own son and focused on the problem at hand.

"You want to know what to say to the press, Mayor?" He fought the urge to sneer, knowing too well the power of the press and their long-range camera lenses. Instead he summoned his best Sports Network smile and lowered his voice a notch so that only the portly politician could hear. "Frankly, Mr. Mayor, I don't—"

"Luke!" Pastor Mills's fingers clapped his shoulder while a set of keys dropped into his hand.

"Dan," Justine said on a thick breath of air. "I'm so glad you're here."

"Trouble?" Dan asked Justine. He wore one of those concerned pastor looks.

Justine nodded, and a look passed between them. As if the preacher could read her mind, he gave her a nod and a smile. Instantly, Luke felt her relax.

"I've made a big mess of things. The whole town's just found out about Brian." One of the film crew shouted a greeting and another held a camera high above the crowd. Justine's lower lip began to tremble. "I should have listened to your advice. Instead I gave in to my pride and kept my secret. Now look what's come of it."

The grip on Luke's shoulder tightened. "Listen, Luke," he said in a barely audible whisper. "Go through the side entrance to the old church, down the hall to the left, and out the back door. My car's parked under the live oak next to the building."

"Look, I—"

"You don't have time to argue. It's the green sedan. You need to get Justine out of here."

Luke gave the mayor one last hard look, the kind he used to use on opposing defensive linemen just before he made them look like idiots. As his former principal began to cringe, Luke turned his back and faced Dan Mills once more.

Exchanging the pastor's keys for the ones to the Harley, he slipped them into Dan's palm. When the pastor expressed confusion, Luke said, "You might need a ride." He indicated the parking lot next to the café, now teeming with people. "Mine's the black one."

Despite the gravity of the situation, Dan smiled. "Thanks, but I'll just hold onto these until you need them," he said as he looked past Luke to his secretary. "Justine, with your permission, I'd like to say a few words about gossip and the golden rule to the good folks on First Street."

"Yes, thank you," she said.

Dan turned to face the politician and the crowd. "Mayor," the pastor said in his no-nonsense, Sunday services voice, "shall we do something about this mess? I believe I can clear up this whole misunderstanding with just a few words of explanation."

Luke jerked Justine into motion and propelled her past the few brave souls who dared to stand in their way. Moments later, they dove into the pastor's dark green, conservative, family sedan.

Doors locked and windows darkened, he found himself completely alone with her in the expansive interior of the pastor's car. The silence roared between them, deafening and uncomfortable until he cranked the ignition and the radio snapped to life. A sappy commercial for a piano rental company gave way to soft classical music as Justine snapped her seat belt into place.

"I'm sorry," she whispered, her moist baby blues not quite meeting his stare. "I wanted to tell you, but not like that."

I wanted to tell you.

Not like that.

There's nothing to tell, he wanted to say.

Buying time, Luke eased the tan leather seat back a few inches to give his legs some room, then adjusted the steering wheel to fit him. Before he could speak, a wave of pain sliced through his chest and knocked him back against the seat. A guttural noise, his own voice, slammed against the inside of his head and echoed against his brain.

The disease was catching up, moving quicker than he thought. In the three years since his diagnosis he'd only had a handful of episodes like this one. Each one hit him harder, and the interim between them had grown shorter and shorter.

All signs pointed to the inevitable. Like his father and brother before him, his defective heart was about to give up.

"Luke?"

Justine's voice floated toward him as images of her swirled around him. Nausea rose in his throat, and breathing became almost impossible. Soon, it would be over.

"Luke? What's wrong?"

Nearer this time, she spoke in a more urgent tone. He gasped for breath and found cold, clear air. Coughing, he pressed the pain into submission with the palm of his hand as his cardiologist in Houston had taught him to do. Justine's face hovered at the edge of his line of sight and gradually came into focus as the last of the discomfort subsided.

"Oh, praise God, Luke." She clutched at her seat belt and pushed it out of the way to lean toward him. Her soft lips formed a weak smile. "I thought you'd had a heart attack or something."

He should have said "yes." Luke flexed his fingers and inhaled a deep draft of cool air mingled with the scent of leather and Justine's perfume. "I'm fine," he lied.

"But you don't look fine."

Another wrench of pain stabbed at his chest, and he doubled over. His head hit the steering wheel with a thud, and a split second later he felt like the entire Denver Broncos defensive line had landed on him at once.

Justine pressed her cool palm against his forehead, bringing her close, too close. Luke shut his eyes and forced his breathing to regulate. His hands began to shake, so he gripped the steering wheel to hide their tremor.

"You're clammy," she said. "I think you need to see a doctor. Why don't we trade places, and I'll take you over to the ER?"

Blinking back the pain waiting just below her fingers, Luke encircled her wrist with his hand and removed it from his forehead. He slid a hand inside his shirt pocket and fished out the vial containing his medication. Before he swallowed a pill, he forced a smile. "I am fine," he repeated, enunciating each word with care.

While he worked the capsule down his throat, he studied Justine and her severe hairstyle. The little knot of hair at the back of her neck looked worse than the braid she'd worn yesterday. What was wrong with her? The Justine Kane he knew always wore her hair loose and free. Back then it had suited her well, and since the years had been more than kind to her, it most likely still did.

His fingers itched to loosen it and see the golden strands fall across her shoulder.

Across his shoulder.

Luke gulped, more from surprise at the random thought than the pain still coursing through him at regular intervals.

"Okay," drifted softly toward him across the wide expanse of the front seat. It sounded more like a question than an answer.

He took several slow breaths, letting each of them out slowly as he willed away any more twisted thoughts of Justine along with any further thoughts of his demise. As the medication kicked in and his pulse moderated, his temper increased.

How could he possibly be the father of any child by snooty little Justine Kane? The odds were staggeringly high against it. Even if it were somehow true, in a town the size of Bailey's Fork, a pregnant teenager would definitely have been noticed.

Someone would have said something, and somewhere along the way it would have gotten back to him. It's not like no one knew where to find him.

He disentangled his fingers from the steering wheel and slammed his fists on his knees. Every nerve ending between his chest and his head complained at the sudden motion, but he ignored them. There could only be one reasonable explanation for her outrageous statement.

"It's obvious you lied back there, Justine." He leaned back against the seat. "Was it for money or just for the attention?"

"Lied?" Her eyes widened. "How dare you think that!"

He looked her square in the eye and dared her to attempt

another lie. She stared right back at him, and for a moment, he almost believed her story.

Almost, but not quite.

How stupid could he be? He'd come to town with money and a measure of fame, and he'd come back to show it all off to her. How else could a small-town girl like Justine catch the notice of a man like him but by making up an outlandish story like this?

He managed a brief smile before the corners of his mouth became too heavy. Even as he let them drop, he felt his spirit soar past the last remnant of pain his body felt. Things were happening as he'd planned after all; he just hadn't planned for them to move quite this fast.

"Darlin', you and I both know it only happened once." He made another attempt at a smile and almost succeeded. "And I'm not so sure it happened then."

Anger glinted in her eyes, but she said nothing. Luke shook his head to clear his mind and returned his hands to the wheel. Out of the corner of his eye he caught the glint of metal and turned to see a camera crew rounding the corner of the old church building.

"This is my fault, Luke." Justine swiped at her cheek, then had the audacity to lay her damp hand over his. "I should have told you the right way at the right time instead of—"

"Not now," he said as he wrestled his hand away and adjusted the rearview mirror. In it, he caught a glimpse of several men with cameras and a woman with a spotlight heading toward the rear bumper of the car.

"But none of this would have happened if I had been able to control my temper. I am so—"

"Shut up and put your seat belt back on," he said as the first flash went off, followed in rapid succession by three more.

"I don't know what it is about you," Justine said as she buckled herself back in, totally oblivious to the media circus forming on their bumper. "It just seems like every time you and I are—"

"Justine, stop talking and hold on," he ground out as he threw the car into gear and pressed the accelerator. "And do something about that hair."

"What's wrong with my—oh!"

The car shot out of the parking lot and bumped into the alley behind First Street. The pain jolted him, but not as fiercely as before. The episode had nearly subsided.

"I told you to hold on," he said as he steered the car out of the narrow alley and onto the street. His heart settled into an even rhythm, as the pain faded to nothing and disappeared. It appeared he would live to fight another day.

"Now what were you saying, Darlin'?"

"I asked you what was wrong with my hair. Ouch!" she shouted as the car hit a pothole on Elm Street.

Luke checked the road behind him. So far, no one had followed. He pulled to the curb on the corner of Third and Elm.

"Thank goodness I survived," she said as she released the seat belt. "I'll just walk home from here, and we can talk about this tomorrow. Is noon okay?"

She released the door lock and reached for the handle. Anticipating her move, Luke pressed the power lock, then reached toward her. If the two of them were going to spend some quality time together today, one thing had to go.

"Hey! What are you doing?"

"I told you to do something about your hair."

Luke fisted a handful of Justine's hair, gently reaching beneath the silky strands to pull out the pins securing the awful hairdo in place. Her hair fell in waves over her shoulders and covered the back of his hand in a blanket of softness.

"That's better." He forced himself to pull away and toss the pins out the window. In the rearview mirror, a car came into view. "Now hold on."

While Justine scrambled to try and release her seat belt, Luke hit the gas. She fell back against the seat and scowled.

"Must you drive like Miss Emma?"

"I'm going to ignore that," he said. "Now sit back and enjoy the ride."

"Ride? My house is just—Luke, where are you going?"

He ignored her.

"Luke?"

Again, he said nothing.

"All right, Luke, this isn't funny."

"No," he said as he signaled to turn left, "it's not. But then I'm not laughing, am I, Darlin'?"

Justine sighed. "I was just a kid, and you weren't around, Luke. I need you to understand this. Please?"

He gave her a look to show her how little her words had affected him. It was a stretch, since each one of them twisted inside his mind and lodged in his heart, but he tried.

"Luke?"

"I'd appreciate it if you'd just refrain from talking while I make sure we've lost our camera crew."

Would she ever stop? She could tell him nothing he needed to know. Once she realized his true plans for Bailey's Fork, she would understand how little he cared.

She would also understand just why the prodigal had returned.

ten

After driving around in circles for what seemed like an eternity but was actually a matter of minutes, Luke quietly deposited Justine at her front door, leaving her with nothing to do but think about the mess she'd created.

And such a mess! She realized this with painful clarity the next day when she snapped on the television and saw her face on the evening news. Stricken, she sank onto the sofa and pressed the mute button on the remote. She watched, horrified, as the camera panned from her to the crowd outside the café and finally to Luke, who stood motionless in a crowd of moving bodies. His expression contorted, then quickly recovered. The camera swung over to the mayor and the ladies and gentlemen of the town who had been fortunate enough to witness the spectacle she'd caused.

Justine turned off the television and dropped the remote control. Now what? She rested her head on the back of the sofa and closed her eyes. What an afternoon it had been. Today she'd felt the stares of a few on the way to work and endured the silence of people who would have normally spoken freely in front of her.

In one day she'd gone from saint to sinner, from the dependable church secretary to a woman with a shameful past. And then there was the matter of Luke. And of Brian.

What a mess she'd made of it.

"Lord, I have done it again," she whispered. "I've gone and tried to handle things my way, and what a disaster it has become." She sighed and curled her feet under her, snuggling deeper into the soft cushions of the sofa. "Help me undo the damage. Help me to follow You. . . ."

A verse from Proverbs crossed her heart and she said it aloud. " *'In his heart a man plans his course, but the Lord determines his steps.'* "

Lifting her eyes to heaven, Justine smiled. "If only I would listen."

"Listen to who?"

Justine jumped to her feet and whirled around to see her son filling the doorway. Light spilled around him, silhouetting his lanky blue-jeaned figure. Today he wore a crimson baseball cap and a matching T-shirt, both proclaiming his allegiance to the University of Houston in bold white letters. He pulled off the cap and ran his fingers through his unruly hair in a useless attempt to tame it.

"Brian," she exclaimed and ran to envelop him in her arms. "I'm so glad you're here. I thought I'd have to wait until tomorrow to see you."

"Mom, you act as if the prodigal son has returned," he said, lifting her easily off her feet for a bear hug. When he placed her on the floor again, he shook his head and offered a crooked grin. "It's just plain old me," he said slowly, the evidence of his Texas roots flowing through each word. "Nothing special."

She held him at arm's length and let her gaze fall to his broad smile, his upturned nose, and finally to his father's blue-green eyes. So wonderful, this young man. Such a tribute to the Lord that He had allowed her to give birth to him. And such a tribute to the parents who raised him that he had a strong Christian faith.

Part of her heart ached at what she had missed. What had he been like as a child? Had he eaten his vegetables or fed them to the dog as she had? Had he been afraid of monsters under the bed or had he fearlessly slept in the arms of the Lord?

So much had still been left unspoken between them. The boy before her had been a man long before she had become his mother. Now at well over six feet, he was still her child.

He always would be.

And there would be plenty of time to know everything. That is, if he could forgive her for not telling her the one thing she should have said from the beginning. That he had a father as well as a mother.

"Oh, Honey, you will never be just plain Brian," she said, burying her face against his broad shoulder once more. "You are my miracle child."

His grip tightened around her. "Wow, you're easy to please," he said in the offhanded way she'd come to love.

She inhaled the faint scent of something familiar, something she didn't associate with her son. "Ivory soap," she whispered against his chest when she identified the fragrance.

Her heart soared and sunk. She bit back the urge to cry.

"What?" Brian asked.

"I said you smell like soap." She broke off the embrace and linked her arms with his. Mustering all the cheer she could manage, she lifted her chin and met his questioning gaze. "Come in and sit down, Honey. Are you hungry?" She released his arm and made a turn toward the kitchen. "Well, of course you're hungry," she muttered. "How about a sandwich? I think I've still got some—"

Brian chuckled and made a grab for her. His fingers encircled her wrist, halting both her conversation and her progress.

"Contrary to what you might think, I am no longer a growing boy, Mom. I'm almost twenty. I don't need to be fed every waking moment."

She returned his laugh with one of her own and patted his hand. Her gaze fell to his long legs and his feet, currently encased in a rather large pair of hiking boots that looked eerily familiar.

Again she pushed away the comparison to Luke. Better to think of only Brian today. Tomorrow would come soon enough.

"I suppose if you grew any more we'll have to put an extension on the guest room bed," she said lightly.

"Well, it's funny you should mention the guest room." Brian released her wrist, then quickly captured her hand between his. He met her gaze before he quickly ducked his head. "Because I was wondering if you might consider letting me flop there for awhile."

"Flop?" Recognition dawned, and with it the twin feelings of elation and dread. "You mean stay here? With me?"

"I thought I might get a job around here for the summer. You know, spend more time with you." He paused, looking unsure. "If it's all right with you."

Her son living under her roof? How would the good citizens of Bailey's Fork treat him—or her?

Justine squared her shoulders and chastised herself for caring about something so inconsequential. Only the Lord Almighty had the power to decide what was right, and she felt pretty sure He would be quite pleased with the arrangement.

"Is it all right?" She launched herself into his embrace for the third time. "Honey, it's more than all right."

"I was hoping you would say that."

He squeezed her so hard her breath froze in her throat.

Just when she'd almost recovered, he did it again.

She tucked her head under his chin and closed her eyes. The faint scent of Ivory soap once again assailed her. She ignored it.

"What else would I say?"

"I just thought that. . ." Brian paused.

Justine looked up into eyes full of doubt. "What?"

"Oh, I don't know." He shook his head. "You haven't tried to hide me or anything, so it's not that, but. . ." Again, he stopped.

She knew where he was headed with this line of questioning, but she also knew he needed to be the one to say it. She'd already come to a decision; now it was his turn.

"But?"

"But I might come as a surprise to some people. You're the church secretary after all. I don't want to make things hard on you."

"Brian, if anyone has a problem, they will need to take it up with the Lord, won't they?"

"I love you, Mom," he said against the top of her head.

It took her an eternity to recover, but when she did, the words poured out along with an unspoken but heartfelt thanks to the Lord. "Oh, Honey," she said loud enough for the neighbors to hear. "I love you too."

❧

Outside on the lawn, Luke stood in impassive silence as he watched his old girlfriend wrap herself around a kid young enough to deliver newspapers for a living. Rage seethed in his veins, and the need to break something bore hard on his mind.

To think he'd actually come here to apologize to Justine for the way he had treated her on the ride home. He'd even considered relenting and letting her run the senior center project. And he'd toyed with believing her crazy story about him fathering her child.

Of course, that one was a real stretch.

He shook his head. His decision to make things right with Justine had been impulsive, and he realized it the minute her house had come into view. With her nosy neighbor standing guard at the edge of the fence, he'd circled around the block to approach from the opposite side, then thought better of the whole thing and decided to go home. If only he had.

But then he spied Justine through the front window. From where he stood, it looked like she was crying. He hadn't anticipated that. From there it had all gone downhill. As he balled his fingers into fists and fought the urge to punch something, he tried to decide how things had gone so wrong.

It had definitely started with his decision to watch Justine for just a moment longer while he contemplated his options. She seemed to glance his way, and he remembered shifting positions and crowding closer to the side of the garage between the hedge and the wall. When the big red truck barreled into her driveway just a few feet ahead of him, he realized he could either leave or stick around to see what would happen next. With music blasting from the truck's open windows and college and fraternity stickers on the back, Luke surmised the driver must be young and male. He decided to stick around.

"Probably pizza delivery," he muttered. He'd already determined Justine was not a prize-winning chef by the contents of her kitchen. Likely, she ordered food delivery quite a lot, although in a town the size of Bailey's Fork, the pickings most likely were slim.

Maybe someday he'd invite her to sample some of his

cooking. Adam's favorite, chicken salad, would be the first because it was the best and easiest. They could make it together; she'd really be impressed with his abilities then.

Of course, she probably didn't own a decent pot or pan, so he'd have to bring his own. Maybe he'd buy her a set so he could cook there whenever he felt like it. Then she would see that not only could he cook, but he could also afford the best utensils.

Luke shook his head and sent the stupid idea flying. Right now he couldn't concentrate on what he *might* do; he had to think of what he *would* do. The first thing that came to mind was to stay hidden and bide his time until the coast was clear. *Until Joe College gets his pizza money and leaves.*

Peering out through the cover of the branches, he watched the long-legged kid spill out of the truck and head for the back door like he owned the place. Luke studied the kid in an impartial manner and decided he wasn't bad looking, in a college athlete sort of way.

Strange, though, something seemed familiar about him. Before Luke could figure out what that something was, the guy had the nerve to stroll right in Justine's back door without so much as a knock.

Curiosity got the best of him, and Luke slid around the corner to find a better hiding spot, one between the climbing purple wisteria vine and the front porch. From that angle, he watched as the kid stood in the kitchen for an eternity while Justine sat with her back to him on the sofa, eyes closed and lips moving as if in conversation.

Didn't she know a guy stood less than twenty feet from her? What if he meant her harm? What if Joe College was some loony-toon who preyed on lonely women who lived alone?

Luke took a step toward the front door, then froze when Justine jumped, gave a shout of joy, and ran toward the kid like a defensive tackle bent on stopping the quarterback. She wrapped her arms around the guy and held on like there was no tomorrow.

Like she used to hold on to me.

Irritation kicked in. A few minutes later, she and Joe College began to laugh like a couple of kids on the playground, and his feelings blossomed into full-fledged anger. The urge to hit something bore too hard on him, and reliving the whole incident just made it worse. His anger exploded into action when he heard Justine's gleeful shout and expression of love.

The first thing Luke broke was the clay pot of red geraniums by the front door. The second thing he broke was the front door itself.

"Luke, what have you done?" he heard Justine say just before he landed at her feet.

eleven

What had he done?

For the first time in his life, Luke felt like a prize-winning fool. There had been a hundred times when he'd done stupid things, but never once had he worried much about them or their consequences. Stuff happened, people got over it.

But this was different.

He should say something, anything, to explain why he now stood inside Justine's house instead of out on the sidewalk or, better yet, back home where he belonged.

Justine stood, open-mouthed, while the kid advanced on him. Only his slight advantage in height kept Luke upright as he sidestepped Joe College like the football star he had been. Before he could enjoy his victory, the walls tilted and his head hit the floor.

A sea of crimson blocked his vision, and a heavy weight crossed his chest. Luke could only watch as sparks of light bounced off the edges of his vision and reflected against bright white letters spelling the word Houston. Blood pumped fast in his veins and roared in his ears. Strangely, the familiar weakness of his heart did not appear, although the weight remained.

"Brian! Let him go!" Justine shouted through the din. "I know him."

The weight lifted as the wall of red moved, and Justine's face took its place. He blinked hard, and clear vision returned.

While she didn't smile, Justine didn't exactly look angry, either. He made the absurd observation that she still wore her hair down the way he liked it and that the soft cascade of tawny hair fell across her shoulder as she leaned over him. He stared at it rather than at her.

"What's the matter, Luke?" she finally asked. "Cat got your tongue?"

When he didn't answer, she looked past him to the kid. "Help him up," she said.

Grudgingly, Joe College grasped him by the wrist and gave a hard tug. Luke flew upright and landed on his feet, barely, for the force of his climb almost sent him reeling forward. For a relatively skinny kid, he sure had some power in his arms.

Luke met the youth's angry glare. Familiarity struck him again. Somewhere between the proud chin and the furrowed dark brows lay a face he knew.

"Brian, this is Luke Butler," Justine said, interrupting the thought. "He's an old friend of mine from high school."

The kid's eyes widened. "Hey, are you *the* Luke Butler? Oh man, I used to watch you play when I was a kid. You used to be the greatest."

Ouch. That hurt worse than the collision.

"Luke," Justine said, "this is Brian Brown." She paused, and her baby blues narrowed. "The young man I told you about today."

The young man I told you about today.

He shook off the comment along with the reminder of his advanced age and offered Joe College, now named Brian Brown, his hand. Again, his grip felt surprisingly strong.

"Pleased to meet you, Sir," he said in the thickest Texas accent Luke had ever heard. "Sorry about the. . ." He paused, looking sheepish as he continued to pump Luke's hand. "About knocking you to the floor. I didn't know you were *the* Luke Butler. I thought you were some kind of loony-toon." He ducked his head.

"No problem. About the door," he said, releasing Brian's hand. "I should explain."

"Yes, you should," Justine said evenly.

Okay, Luke, old boy. Time to lay it on thick. Open your mouth and lie your way out of this one.

But when he tried, nothing came out.

Every great excuse he'd planned evaporated in one huge cloud of honesty. "I saw you tangled up with Brian here, and the next thing I knew I was inside instead of outside."

Where had those words come from?

A tiny voice, a soft mingling of peace and comfort, teased his ear. *"An honest answer is like a kiss on the lips."*

He looked from Brian to Justine. Neither gave any indication they had heard anything.

"Luke, are you all right?"

He nodded. But was he? First he'd come crashing through Justine's door, and now he'd actually admitted he'd been spying on her. It seemed as though someone, or something, wanted him to make a fool of himself in front of Justine and her guest. *"The Lord sustains the humble,"* the voice said, again lacing the words with quiet serenity.

Luke tugged at his ear and regarded Justine with what he hoped would be a casual smile. "You know it's the funniest story how this happened, actually. See, it all started when. . ."

He stopped. The words had left, and along with them his pride had followed.

"Luke, why don't you sit down? You don't look well," Justine said. She turned to Brian. "Do you mind getting Mr. Butler a glass of water?"

Brian shook his head. "I don't think he needs water, Mom. He looks like he needs a doctor."

Luke sank onto the nearest surface, the first riser of the staircase, while the word worked its way through his brain. The kid had actually called Justine "Mom."

This did not fit into his view of things.

Even now Justine was still young and beautiful and not the mother of anyone. Least of all someone the size of Brian. He gave the kid another look.

The dark hair, the eyes. . .were they blue or green? Oh, who cared? Brian Brown was not Justine's son. He didn't even look like her.

Not a bit.

Against his better judgment, he continued to think. Maybe he did favor her a little around the mouth and somewhat in the area of the nose.

But her hair was as blond as straw, and Brian's was dark. And her eyes were a blue so startling that he'd have noticed if the kid shared the same color. Still, if a person stared long enough at the kid's chin, one could possibly argue the case for a resemblance.

Luke shook his head.

It just couldn't be possible. She had to be Brian's girl, his woman, his. . .

Anyone but his mother.

Brian returned with a glass of ice water and shoved it in Luke's direction. He reached for it and missed, leaving his hand to fall helplessly into his lap. The kid placed the water on the table and nudged Justine with his elbow.

"See, I told you he didn't need water, Mom."

Luke raised his gaze to the ceiling. Again, Brian had called her Mom. Vaguely, he heard Justine explaining the events of the previous afternoon's road trip to the kid, conveniently leaving out the big announcement on First Street.

"He did look kind of ill at one point before we left," she said. "Do you think he might be suffering from shock?"

"I don't think it's shock," Brian said slowly. "You say he drove you home?"

She nodded.

"Well, he's not going to drive you home, take a car back to the pastor, spend a day feeling fine, come back here, come charging through the front door, and *then* go into shock." He shook his head. "Just doesn't work that way." The kid turned to Luke. "My girlfriend's second-year pre-med in psychology," he said confidently. "I help her study."

"Oh yeah?" Luke managed. "That's great."

Luke tried to continue his line of thought about Brian, who now claimed he had a girlfriend, and about Justine, who still acted like the kid was her son, and about his connection between the two of them, and yet found he could not concentrate. Even the soft little voice with all the good advice stayed silent.

"I should go," he mumbled. "The door. Send me a bill. Oh yeah, and I owe you some flowers too."

He'd almost made it to the door when Justine linked her arm with his and brought him to an immediate halt. "How about we call it even?"

She led him back inside and down the hall to the kitchen. Brian trotted along behind her like an obedient puppy, the water glass once again in hand.

"For the grass I ran through at your place," she said in answer to his questioning look. "I had a little trouble with my car. Drove it right into Luke's front yard," she tossed over her shoulder to Brian.

Finally, Justine released him and indicated two chairs at

the kitchen table. "Sit down, please, both of you," she said softly.

"What's up?" Brian asked, obviously unaware of the tension.

"I really need to go," Luke said, surprised by his pure unadulterated fear of having the conversation he knew Justine wanted to have.

Her grip on his arm caught once more and tightened. "This has been twenty years in the making, Luke Butler."

Easily, he extricated himself from her grasp. Before he could speak, the voice returned. *"Be still and know I am the Lord,"* it whispered.

"Oh, that is ridiculous," he said, fighting the rising panic.

Why now, of all the times in his life when he could have used a message from the Man Upstairs, did He choose to reveal Himself? That is, if this was the Lord after all. Maybe Justine was right. Maybe he was in shock.

"I'll tell you what's ridiculous," she said, cutting into his thoughts. "Me letting you leave this room without hearing what I've got to say, now that is ridiculous." Justine flipped a long strand of wheat-colored hair over her shoulder and met his stare with one exactly like it. "What are you afraid of, Luke?"

Before he could answer, Justine's sister, her four kids, and Hank Hawthorn piled through the back door unannounced, all chattering at once. When the clamor died down to a mild roar, the youngest of the bunch, a red-haired charmer with big green eyes, shouted, "Aunt Justine, you're never gonna guess what happened at the Bowl-A-Rama tonight!"

twelve

"Momma and Hank took us bowling," the little darling continued, her hands moving nearly as fast as her mouth. A second later, she launched herself into Justine's embrace. "And he wrote it on the bowling pins."

Justine wrapped her arms around the girl and gently kissed her freckled forehead. "Slow down, Lainey. I don't speak ten-year-old so well anymore." She settled one of the child's fiery red curls back into place. "Now tell me. What did Uncle Hank write on the bowling pins?"

Hank and Abby slipped in, arms linked. Once inside, Hank removed his University of Houston cap and playfully tossed it at Brian. The kid missed the catch, another indication to Luke that Brian Brown could be no child of his. Any kid carrying the Butler genes would have caught it.

Luke turned to examine Justine's sister. A few years older than Justine, with hair the color of copper, Abby bore an eerie resemblance to her mother. Luke quickly looked away but found his gaze strayed back to her. As far as he knew, Mrs. Kane had wished him no ill will, but neither had she supported his cause with Justine. The memory burned, and he swallowed hard to force it into submission.

"But he's not gonna be my uncle Hank anymore," the little one continued. "He's gonna be my—"

"Hey guys, Mr. Butler and Aunt Justine have a lot to talk about." Abby stared in his direction. He saw no kindness there. "Why don't we do this later?" Her attention moved to Brian and with it her look softened. "Hiya,

Cutie," she said. "Sure glad you're here."

"Hi, Aunt Abby," Brian said, then continued with something about architecture class and a girlfriend.

Finally he paused to stare at Luke. For a moment, Luke felt as if the young man were sizing him up, as if he were protecting Justine for some reason. It felt strange, and yet Luke had to admire the kid for his devotion.

"And I'll be staying with Mom this summer," he said.

Mom. There was that word again. Luke cleared his throat and tried not to think.

Hank cleared his throat as well. "So anyone want to talk me out of marrying the redhead?"

"Marry?" Justine squealed. "Did you ask Abby to marry you?"

He nodded.

"And she said yes?" Justine asked.

Again, he nodded. This time Abby joined him.

Justine squealed and headed for her sister. The pair locked arms, while Hank wisely took a couple of steps back and gave them room. "I can't believe it," Justine said. "This is wonderful."

Abby began to giggle. "I know, but when a man writes 'Marry me' on bowling pins and has the alley set them up that way, what're you going to say?"

Justine embraced her sister and gathered the ten year old into the circle. "Oh, that's so romantic."

Romantic? Idiotic was more like it.

Luke calculated the odds of escaping under the cover of the chaos, but he quickly discarded the idea when a pair of red-haired teenage boys, obviously twins, sauntered in from outside and planted themselves squarely in the doorway. Instantly they began to push and poke each other. Another child, a fair-haired girl who looked to be about twelve, studied Brian openly.

"Guess they heard," the girl commented. She took a seat next to Brian at the table and continued to stare at him.

Hank strolled toward Luke with a crooked grin, tossing a quick glance over his shoulder at the mob of women and children in the kitchen. "You probably think I'm crazy, wanting to get saddled with this bunch."

Brian retrieved Hank's hat and fitted it atop the girl's blond head. "Here ya go, Tina," he said with a grin. "How's things in the seventh grade?"

She squealed and threw the cap toward the twins, who then began a game of keep-away with it. Through it all, the little one never stopped talking and the sisters never stopped hugging.

Despite all the confusion, they looked like the family Luke never had. The family he should have had. *Where had that come from?* Luke extended his hand. "Hey, congratulations."

"Thanks." Hank ducked his head and nodded as he clasped Luke's hand. "Looks like between marrying into this bunch and fixing up Lakeside so it's livable, I'm going to have my hands full."

"You mean you're actually planning to live out at the Lakeside Cabins? I thought you were buying it as an investment."

He nodded. "It is an investment, in my future, that is. I'm looking for someone to manage the delivery business full time, but until then, I'm going to have to keep at it."

"I guess that makes sense."

"Yeah, and it's a great place to raise kids. That's the main reason I bought it." Hank gestured toward the twins. "Those boys lost their daddy when they were three. They have no idea what it's like to live out in the country and hunt and fish. Don't you think it's high time they learned?"

Luke nodded and swallowed the lump forming in his throat.

"This crew's why I thought turning Lakeside Cabins into a big old house in the country would be a good idea. I figured I could put in a Christian campground downriver a bit, and me and Abby could manage the place." He grinned. "Leastwise, that's what I was thinking when I bought it."

Lakeside would be a perfect place to live. Though the huge main building sorely needed repair, it hugged a beautiful lake, and the seven outlying cabins stood among a grove of longleaf pines in some of the nicest land in the county. He knew because he'd tried to buy it himself, only to find Hank had beat him to it.

"You mean you planned this all along?" He gave Justine and her sister another glance, then quickly looked away. "Marrying into the Kanes, I mean."

"Oh yeah."

"You're a brave man, Hank Hawthorn."

Hank smiled. "I've had my sights set on Abby ever since I set eyes on her in church. She raised her kids all by herself after their daddy died, you know."

"Really?" He thought about his mother, and how she raised him after his father died. Too bad she hadn't lived long enough to finish the job.

"Sure," Hank said. "When the Lord put it on my heart she was the one for me, it was just a matter of time before I gave in and let Him lead me. She's quite a woman."

While Hank smiled at Abby, Luke chanced another look at Justine. "Yes, she *is* quite a woman."

Justine continued her conversation with Abby and the girls, never realizing he'd looked her way. Regretfully,

Luke's attention returned to Hank.

"But I'm gonna need a place to house 'em all while I'm fixing up Lakeside," he said slowly. "Guess I'll just have to see if they can fit one more over in the cracker box Abby calls a house."

"Hey, I'm not unpacked yet," Luke commented.

This much was true. Other than the furniture that had come with the house and the food he'd had delivered last weekend, his only concession to home ownership had been to purchase a garden hose at Sears. Why he'd bothered, he had no idea. Perhaps it had been because in all the years he'd lived, this place had been the first to feel like a home. And for some reason, homes were supposed to have things like big green garden hoses.

"Luke, you all right?" Hank asked. "You look a little green around the gills."

He shook his head and cleared the errant thoughts from his mind. "Yeah, I'm fine," he answered quickly. Carefully avoiding Justine's gaze, he smiled at Hank. "Look, this is a special occasion. Why don't I just let you folks celebrate the good news?"

Before he could move, Justine wrapped an arm around his. "This is the answer to a prayer," she said, looking at Abby and not him. "I'm so happy for you."

Lainey began to chatter again, but Abby put a quick stop to it with a firm hand on her shoulder. "Honey, we can tell Aunt Justine all about this tomorrow." She gave her a playful shove in the direction of the girl who sat staring at Brian. "Tina, say good-bye to your cousin, then take your sister to the car."

Abby turned toward the back door, then cast a long look at Justine over her shoulder. "See *you* tomorrow," she said and pressed her palm to the little one's back to hurry her along. Justine released Luke to hug her sister and offer another round of congratulations to the future bride and groom.

While Justine's sister reined in the two girls, Hank Hawthorn had the good sense to shepherd the boys out into the yard. "Bye, Brian," Tina called as she disappeared around the edge of the porch.

A second later, Hank appeared in the door. "What have I done?" he asked playfully before snagging his cap from the floor and bounding back out the door.

What have I done?

Hank's words echoed in Luke's head, and their sentiment echoed in his heart. He inched toward the back door and considered the thought. What had he done?

Justine linked her arm with his once more. "We'll talk out on the porch."

Helpless to resist, he followed as she led them outside to a place near the climbing roses. When she sat, he did the same, and so did Brian. Together they formed a tight circle in the shade of the old trellis. Luke took a deep breath and held the scent of the roses in his lungs as long as he could. When Justine grasped his hand, he expelled the breath.

"Brian already knows most of this story," Justine said softly. "But because I haven't been completely truthful, he doesn't know it all."

Luke felt his fears magnify as the urge to flee pressed hard. He curled Justine's fingers into his palm and held them there.

"The summer of my sixteenth birthday, I stayed with my sister Abby in Dallas instead of spending those three months in Bailey's Fork," Justine said in a voice barely above a whisper. "When I didn't come back until the middle of September, my mother wrote a note to the school explaining I had mono and couldn't return until I was well. What they didn't know. . ." She paused. "What no one knew was that I had delivered a beautiful seven-pound, four-ounce dark-haired son the last day of August."

She flipped a strand of hair over her shoulder and fixed her gaze on Brian. "I never forgot you. You found me, and you loved me even though I had no right to expect it." Brian opened his mouth to speak, but she silenced him with a lift of her hand. "We're a family, you and I, and that's because you found me when I didn't have the courage to find you."

Her baby blues shifted to Luke. Strangely, the urge to run evaporated.

"And Luke is the part of us that has been missing." She grasped Brian's hand and held it in her lap. "He's your father, Sweetheart."

Her other hand tightened around Luke's fingers. He followed the line of her hand up her arm and finally to her face, where a tear shimmered at the corner of one eye.

"Oh, Luke, you've had an amazing life, and you've done so much," she said. "You've had fame and fortune, and a life you never could have lived here in Bailey's Fork."

The truth of the statement stung. He tried in vain to ignore it.

"Luke, I loved you enough to let you go live that life." She looked at Brian once more. "Just like I loved Brian enough to do the same thing for him. Brian, my heart broke when I kissed you for the last time and handed you to your new mom and dad, but I know it was the right thing to do."

Justine held Brian's hand next to Luke's. From the

curve of their thumbs to the size of their palms, the similarities were startling.

Slowly, Luke gathered the courage to look at Brian. A pair of eyes much like his own stared back in defiance, daring him to speak and yet seeming to beg him to say the right thing. Somehow he gathered Justine in his arms and held her against his chest. His heart beat strong and steady, but his gut felt as though it had captured a thousand butterflies.

To his surprise, Brian thrust his free hand toward Luke. The tears in his eyes matched Luke's.

"Mr. Butler, Sir," Brian said slowly, his Texas accent thick as syrup and rough as nails. "It's a pleasure to finally meet you."

Luke's fingers tightened around the kid's hand just as his throat threatened to close. "It sure is. . ." He paused and tested the word in his mind before finally speaking it aloud. "Son," he somehow managed through the tears.

thirteen

"Son." Brian smiled. "Sir, do you have any idea how long I've waited to hear that? From my birth father, that is?"

Luke swallowed the lump in his throat and managed a smile of his own. "If I'd known, I would have said it sooner."

"I'll just give you two some time to talk," Justine said.

And talk they did, covering everything from football to childhoods spent in totally different circumstances to the rebellious teenage years, and finally about how it felt to be a child left alone without parents.

"So that's when I got serious about finding my birth mother," Brian said. "I loved my adoptive parents, and they'll always have a special place in my heart, but God gave me two sets of parents, and I felt a strong need to find the other set."

Luke thought back to the day his football coach called him off the field to tell him his mother had died. How different would his life have been if he'd allowed the state to place him with another foster family like they had with Adam? The startling contrast of his life and his brother's begged consideration, but he refused to give in to it. Instead he concentrated his thoughts on Brian.

"Did you think it would fill the void?" he asked. "I mean, were you looking to replace them by finding Justine?"

Brian looked up sharply and shook his head. The conviction in the boy's eyes reminded Luke of Adam. It seemed as though he'd barely grown to know his brother before he'd lost him. First his father, then his mother, and finally Adam. To his mind, there were far too many Butlers passing through the pearly gates.

"Nothing could replace the parents I lost," Brian said, a touch of sadness in the wry smile he wore.

Luke nodded, and silence fell between them. "You never really get over losing them, do you?" He cringed when he realized he'd spoken the question aloud.

Brian stretched his legs and crossed them at the ankles, allowing his hiking boots to hang over the edge of the porch. From where he sat, Luke could tell the kid's legs were nearly as long as his, and his feet looked bigger. This child of his was nearly grown. The thought of it amazed him, and at the same time, filled him with a mixture of wonder and loss.

For what was to come.

For what he had missed.

"I don't think it's about getting over them," Brian said slowly. "I'll never forget my mom or my dad, but it helps knowing where they are and who they're with."

Luke snapped a pink rose off the vine and studied it. "What do you mean?"

"I mean they're in a better place, and someday we'll be together again." Once more, silence fell between them until Brian reached over to touch his sleeve. "You look like you don't believe that."

He thought for a moment, weighing what he knew with what he believed. "Yeah, I do," he finally said, although he'd rather have not said anything at all. "At least it sounds good."

Brian looked thoughtful. "Have you settled the question of your salvation? I mean, God wants us all to be with Him in heaven someday, and the only way to get there is to turn your life over to Him."

"That's a good one." Luke snorted. "Don't know that the Lord's given me a second thought since grade school, and even then I had to take my mama's word for it."

"I'm sorry you think that."

Brian leaned forward and rested his elbows on his knees. His hands rested between his legs, and his eyes focused on something out in the yard while his fingers twitched nervously.

"Sir, you've told me about your life, how hard it was growing up without a dad, then losing your mom. I can see how that could make a man bitter if he didn't have the Lord to lean on." He cast a sideways glance at Luke. "No matter what, He will never leave us nor forsake us."

Luke leaned back and studied the leaves on the rosebush. "You don't know how it was." He met the boy's stare. "You'll never know."

Brian straightened and shook his head. "No, Sir, I won't, but I know this—God can take any situation and use it for His purpose. He can make good out of any bad that's happened. It says so in His Word, in Romans, chapter eight, verse twenty-eight."

Looking at his son, Luke almost believed him. "Is that right?" he commented.

Without a word, Brian stood and walked across the porch to disappear into the kitchen. Before Luke could decide whether to follow him, the boy returned with a book under his arm. He dropped the book into Luke's lap and settled back into the chair beside him.

"What's this?" Luke asked as he turned the well-worn brown leather volume over to read the title. "Holy Bible," he read. Opening the cover, he paused to take in the childish scribble that spelled out his son's name and the year he'd received the book. "You've had this a long time. It must be something special."

"Yeah," Brian answered. "I want you to have it."

"But I. . ." Whatever lame excuse he'd planned evaporated when he looked into the face of his son. "I hate to take something you obviously care a lot about," he said instead.

"I want you to have it," he repeated. Brian's chin quivered, and for a moment Luke could have sworn the boy looked like he would cry. "And I want to tell you about my Savior."

Silence fell between them as Luke wrestled with the conflicting needs to please his son and to escape his lecture. And it would be a lecture, this discussion of religion he'd been asked to endure. In his limited experience with church people, the hard sell always followed the introduction.

But Brian looked so sincere, and their relationship had only just been launched. Surely he could endure a speech or two from the young man whom he hoped would one day call him Father.

"Speak your mind, Boy," he said as he traced the edge of the Bible. "Just don't expect me to agree."

As Brian began, sounds of the afternoon swelled around them, filling the air with the barking of a dog and the happy shouts of children at play. Luke settled back in his chair and listened, at first to the messenger, then reluctantly to the message. Intrigued with the fervor with which the kid spoke, Luke smiled and even asked for a clarification at one point.

"So you're listening," Brian said. "I'm glad."

"I said I would."

Brian went on to explain the concept in question, noting that the Scripture could be found in the tenth chapter of Romans, verse 13. "And you'll think about what I said?" he asked when he finished.

Luke balanced the Bible on the porch rail. "Yeah, I'll think about it." He glanced over at Brian and found him studying the rosebush. "I used to bring your mother flowers from this bush," Luke commented, hoping his ploy to change the subject would work. "Couldn't afford store-bought, but she didn't seem to mind."

"My girl likes roses too," Brian said with a lopsided grin. "I think I'll bring her back a bouquet on Sunday."

"Tell me about her," Luke said. "What's she like?"

"Becky? She's pretty and smart and tough as nails." He gave Luke a serious look. "Like Mom."

"Yeah," Luke said on a rush of expelled breath.

With a flick of his hand, Luke tossed the rose he had picked over the porch rail and watched it disappear into a thick patch of ferns. Slowly, his gaze returned to his son.

Brian nodded, then looked away, obviously troubled. "Can I ask you a question?"

Dread accompanied his casual demeanor. What if Brian had second thoughts? What if he'd decided Luke Butler to be a sorry excuse for a father and wanted nothing to do with him?

"Sure," Luke said, hoping he could find an answer to whatever his son needed to know.

The kid aimed his gaze at Luke. "What are your intentions with my mother?"

"That's a direct question."

Brian tensed his shoulders and looked Luke square in the eyes. "I guess it is."

"I wish I had a direct answer for you, Brian." He studied the toe of his boot and gave it some thought. "If you're asking whether I have any feelings for her, I'd be lying if I told you I didn't. I just don't know what those feelings are right now."

"Did you love her back then? When you made me, I mean."

The question seared a path directly to his heart. Did he? The answer welled up in his throat and nearly didn't escape.

"With all my heart, Brian," he finally whispered. He blinked back the unmanly tears shimmering against his lower lids. "I intended to marry her."

Brian shifted beside him. "And now that you've found each other again?"

Luke gave his eyes a quick swipe with the back of his hand and pressed his palms to his knees. "Only time will tell, Brian, because I sure don't know."

"Fair enough." Brian paused and traced the edge of the porch rail with his thumb. "Can I ask you another one?"

He gave his son a sideways look. With the long rays of afternoon sun slanting through the roses, Luke realized the kid could have been a carbon copy of him at twenty. The thought warmed his heart and scared him to death at the same time. He'd only known of Brian's existence for a brief while, but already he felt the stirring of fatherhood. Worries began to surface, serious concerns about his future and about how he would do justice to the job of being a dad to this fine young man.

"Is the question about your mother?" he asked, forcing his thoughts back to the present.

Brian shook his head.

"All right then. Ask away."

The boy lowered his gaze to the porch floor, then abruptly swung it back to meet Luke's gaze. "I was just wondering. . ." He paused, biting his lip. He seemed to have difficulty speaking. "I was wondering," he continued. "Is it too soon to call you Dad?"

Luke's tearful embrace answered the question without

words. Too soon, Brian leaned away and dusted off his jeans. "I guess I ought to go fix the front door before it gets dark."

Luke stood too. "Let me help you," he said.

"I'll do it." He looked over his shoulder at the kitchen door. "You relax."

Relax? How would he ever manage to do that? His life had been turned upside down and inside out ever since he set foot in Bailey's Fork.

Brian shifted his weight and studied the porch post, giving Luke the distinct impression he struggled with yet another question. "Anything else you want to ask?"

Relief flooded the kid's face. "Actually, there is," he said slowly. "Would you mind if we prayed?"

Prayed?

The question bored into his heart and settled hard in his mind. He hadn't prayed aloud in more than twenty years, not since his mother's death. What would he say? How would he manage a prayer worthy of the moment?

Before he could find a solution to the dilemma, Brian cleared his throat and began to pray. The words came strong and clear, and through a most unmanly shimmer of tears, Luke listened while his son spoke an eloquent prayer of thanks and of hope for the future. When he ended with a prayer for the Lord's protection for their newfound relationship as father and son, all Luke could do was whisper a pathetic "Amen" as Brian cuffed him on the shoulder and ambled off the porch.

Numb, Luke sank onto the porch step and yanked another rose off the vine. With care, he began to pull each petal away from the stem. Before he realized what he'd done, he'd stripped the poor flower. Rose petals lay strewn across the soft gray porch boards.

You love her.

"Yeah, maybe," he whispered. "Now what?"

Now you tell her everything.

"Mind if I join you?"

Luke looked up to see the object of his thoughts standing just inside the screen door holding a pair of mismatched crystal goblets. "Sure," he said with a shrug.

She elbowed the door open and offered him an iced tea. The glass, a combination of frosted dots and shiny squares that made the contents look a shade lighter in places than it actually was, felt heavy in his hand.

Then a memory two decades old nearly bowled him over. He'd taken a goblet just like this from the country club and filled it with flowers from the fancy centerpiece in the main dining room. The stunt nearly got him fired, but the smile on his ladylove's face had been well worth it.

Funny how he remembered the stupidest things. He took a sip of sweet tea and watched the lemon in his glass swirl around and disappear beneath the surface.

Justine sat on the swing, and Luke settled beside her. "Good tea," he said when he could think of nothing else to say.

"Thank you."

"I wonder why Brian left his Bible out here."

Luke expelled a long breath and edged a little farther away. "He didn't." He paused. "He gave it to me."

"Oh." She took another sip of tea. "That was nice of him."

"Yeah."

As the shadows gathered about them, they rocked in comfortable silence. Occasionally they spoke but never said anything of importance beyond comments on the weather and the time of Sunday services at church.

Apparently, Justine could stand it no longer.

"Okay, what did you two talk about?"

She must have sensed she'd treaded on personal ground and regretted the intrusion. She shook her head and held a palm up. "Never mind," she said quickly. "I'm sorry. It's none of my business."

Luke gave her a slow smile. She looked past him to the roses swaying in the soft breeze. When he took her hand in his, she swung her gaze back to her fingers and the larger ones entwined with them.

"Of course it's your business." Luke paused and squeezed her hand. "Most of it, anyway."

Her gaze met his. "What do you mean?"

"I mean there are just some things a father and son don't need to share with a woman." He punctuated the statement with a wicked grin, then quickly sobered and set the tea glass down on the rail. "Look, we cleared up a lot of stuff, okay?"

She nodded.

"And we prayed," he added, almost too casually.

Justine turned slightly to better see his face. "You did?"

"Yeah." The swing creaked as Luke released her hand and leaned forward to rest his elbows on his knees. "Believe me, I'm as surprised as you are."

Her face turned red. "I didn't mean it like that."

"Yes, you did." He met her embarrassed gaze with a lazy grin. "But it's all right."

Justine returned his smile with one of her own. "Okay, maybe I did. I'm sorry."

With a lift of his hand, Luke waved away her apology. In an instant, he frowned. "I need to say a couple of things."

"All right."

He looked away. "Hard things."

Warm fingers wrapped around his, and a feeling of safe

reassurance flowed from them. "All right," she repeated as she placed her tea glass on the windowsill. "I'm a pretty good listener."

Nodding, Luke tightened his grip on her hand and took a deep breath. He let it out slowly and closed his eyes.

"Contrary to what anyone thinks, I didn't come back to Bailey's Fork to be a hero," he said with obvious difficulty.

"But you're doing such wonderful things. The senior center is a dream come true to this town."

He shook his head. "I didn't care about any senior center or anything else. I only came back to even the score."

"What do you mean?"

"My whole life I've planned to get even with the person I blamed for everything bad that ever happened to me." His voice broke, and he seemed to have difficulty continuing. Finally he cleared his throat. "Two people, actually, but one more than the other."

After a long silence, she seemed to choke out her question. "Who?"

"I hated your father first. He never thought I was good enough for you, so I spent my whole career proving him wrong." He blinked hard. "But he's not the one I hated the longest."

Shock seemed almost to keep her from asking, but somehow she must have found the ability to speak. "Who's the other?"

"You."

fourteen

A slow numbness replaced feelings as Justine tried to make sense of Luke's statement. "Why?"

"Because when you didn't have the guts to tell me you didn't care about me anymore, your old man did." Luke shifted positions, and the chains on the swing clanged loudly against each other. His shoulders sagged. "I shouldn't have said that." He rubbed the back of his neck and frowned.

Silence fell between them once more as Justine digested the information. So this is how it had been with Luke. He'd hated her all these years. Righteous indignation rose at the thought, quickly followed by chastisement. She too had felt hate. Funny how they'd both hated the same person.

Her father had done what he felt to be right at the time, and she could find no fault with his taking charge of the situation. Twenty years ago, a girl of sixteen could offer nothing to a child. Her father had known it, even when she had not. No, it was not her father for whom she felt such hate. It was for herself. For what she could have done. And for what she did instead.

"Justine?"

"Yes?"

She slid Luke a sideways glance. He seemed perched on the edge of the swing, an athlete poised to make a record-setting run.

"That was a stupid thing to say." He stood abruptly, shaking the swing with the sudden motion. "Forget about it, okay?"

Forget about it?

Justine blinked back the tears rimming her eyes. How stupid she was to act like such a crybaby. So what if Luke Butler hated her for the last twenty years? With the poor job she'd done of ending their relationship, she deserved no less.

"It's me who should apologize, Luke," she said. "And my father as well." She paused, pondering how much of Arthur Kane's disease Luke needed to know. "If he could, I'm sure he would," she finally said.

Luke gave a snort of disgust. "I doubt that."

"Why?"

"Because I was never good enough." He studied his hiking boots. "I came back here intending to show him just how wrong he was."

"He's in a nursing home," she somehow managed. "It's a nice little place called Shady Acres."

Luke's silence prompted her to continue.

"Alzheimer's disease. He probably won't even know who you are, much less what a wonderful man you've become," she said gently, touching his arm with the tips of her fingers.

With the contact, he snagged Brian's Bible and fairly leaped off the porch. Three steps into the yard, he turned and started to speak. With a shake of his head, he disappeared around the side of the house in several long strides. A few seconds later, he reappeared.

"About the senior center," he said. "You still interested in running the thing?"

She nodded, numb.

"Then the job's yours."

Long after Luke had gone, Justine sat in the swing and watched the slow approach of evening, the sound of

Brian's hammer pounding a soft rhythm on the opposite side of the house. Twilight had always been her favorite time of day.

These moments of time bridging day and night, sunshine and darkness, held an almost magical quality for her. Always, the chirp of the night birds and the soft singing of the cicadas brought back memories. Tonight she allowed them to flow, swirling in bright colors and soft hues until she immersed herself in them and became part of the world time had left behind. . .another twilight evening when she'd ridden away on the back of a motorcycle with a man her father had sworn to hate.

She and Luke had gone to a spot on the shore of Bailey's Lake, in the shadow of the Lakeside Cabins. Carrying a bottle of cheap bourbon and an itchy wool blanket, they'd left Bailey's Fork with nothing more in mind than defying Arthur Kane and his restrictions. They returned early the next morning under the cover of darkness, two kids who had no idea that what they had done would bind them together for life.

A tear trickled down her cheek, quickly followed by many more. How naïve she'd been. The warm night engulfed her, held her in its grasp, and slowly her wet eyes slid shut. Hidden behind her lids rested a picture of Luke, twenty years younger and full of a volatile combination of cocky self-assuredness and too much alcohol. Everything she'd sworn to forget came flooding back. Luke had been angry with her father, and his anger had pushed him to drink. Abruptly her eyes flew open. The night bore in too close, the memory painful. Still it would not leave her.

She could have stopped things before they went too far. But his kisses were so sweet, and the night felt so warm.

They were young and in love.

Justine heard the ragged gasp and realized her lips had formed it. "Someday I'm going to marry you, Darlin'," floated across her thoughts like a whisper.

Married. Luke had spoken the words on that fateful night, and even through the bourbon on his breath, she felt he had meant them. Brian had been the result.

Her son had been conceived in love, and yet when the time came to admit to that love, she couldn't. She had let her father send Luke away with a brusque warning never to return.

Why?

All those years she'd hated herself compounded and compressed into a tight bundle of self-loathing that settled into a lump in her throat. She lifted her eyes to heaven and offered her burden to the Lord.

"Father, I've really messed things up."

And so has Luke, came the gentle answer. *Be patient.*

❧

His patience at an end, Luke stormed through the front door of the Hawthorn house and slammed it behind him. The Bible landed on the table next to the chair with a thud.

Someday he would have to think of this place as his home, but not tonight. Tonight his thoughts gathered and dispersed, refusing to collect into one sane idea worth contemplating, at least nothing not connected in some way to Justine Kane.

Justine.

The mother of his son.

Of all the things he had expected to accomplish in giving up his broadcasting career and moving to Bailey's Fork, gaining a nearly full-grown son had not been one of them. And what of his intentions?

In one fell swoop he had gained a son and lost a goal. How could he carry out his plans now? How could he set up a man for ruin who was his son's grandfather? How could he flaunt the injustice of his leaving Bailey's Fork to a woman who had spent her life making up for his absence?

Luke stepped over an unpacked box and a small mountain of unopened mail and sank into the single comfortable chair in the room. He grabbed the Bible and held it in his hands. To his surprise, it fell open to the book of Romans. Unable to remember the specifics of the verse Brian had quoted, he simply picked a spot at the end of chapter eight and began to read.

"For I am persuaded, that neither death, nor life, nor angels, nor principalities, nor powers, nor things present, nor things to come, nor height, nor depth, nor any other creature, shall be able to separate us from the love of God, which is in Christ Jesus our Lord."

With a sigh, he closed his eyes and crossed both arms over his chest. What a joke. He'd been separated from every love he'd ever had, starting with his father's and mother's, then Justine's, and finally his brother's. How could he believe a love existed that could defy these odds?

While the silence gathered, he gave into the tug Justine held on his thoughts. Like a veteran broadcaster, he replayed the evening in his mind. A picture of Justine formed and gradually focused. Things hadn't exactly turned out like he'd planned. So much for being honest with her.

"What did that get me, Lord?"

His eyes slid open and focused on the telephone. Maybe he should call her.

"And say what?" echoed in the empty house. "I told her I hated her *and* her father."

He had spoken the truth, at least in part. He *had* hated them. Every time he read an article about himself or heard a sportscast where he figured prominently, he heard the voice of old man Kane telling him he was no good. Every time he caught a pass for a touchdown or walked into an end zone ahead of a defender, he saw Justine's face.

Nothing in his life had been good enough to clear the images from his head. Returning to Bailey's Fork had been his last attempt to erase them. His last attempt before his defective heart gave up and the curse of the Butler family took him too.

Systematically, he intended to buy every piece of property where a wrong had been committed against him. Only the old high school had been left off the list of purchases, a concession to the coach who'd taken him under his wing.

In his grand scheme, he envisioned himself as owner of the country club where as a poorly uniformed busboy, he endured the cold stares on Saturday mornings of the same people who cheered for him on Friday nights. The church building had been next, a trophy to show off to the pious souls who sat in the same pew every Sunday and prayed he wouldn't darken their doorsteps or attempt to date their daughters. Finally he'd bought the First Street Bakery and the Hawthorn house. The latter he'd purchased as a place to stay and try to forget, the former as a place to visit and try to remember.

His plan had been moving along quite well until he heard the noise in the attic of the church and had foolishly gone to investigate. With his first glimpse of Justine Kane, covered in dust and cobwebs and more beautiful than he remembered, he was eighteen and tongue-tied all over again.

Not that he'd let her know. Like an idiot, he assumed he could handle Justine and the surge of memories one glance caused. Now he knew he could neither handle her nor forget her.

Only this evening on the back porch of her house, Justine had the nerve to climb out of his head and curl up in his heart. That piece of work sure put a crimp in his plans.

Somewhere between hello and good-bye, things had gone a little off balance. Nothing had been settled with Justine; no great solutions had been found to the complicated maze of feelings and hurts that surrounded them. Instead, he found out he had a son, a good kid who'd turned to college as a way to actually learn something rather than a way to make a quick buck playing football.

A son who accepted him as his father despite his absence.

A son who could pray out loud.

Try it. For your son.

Frightened, Luke flew out of the chair, and the Bible hit the floor. He turned in every direction to find the voice of the intruder, then scooped up his son's book. Unlike the gentle tone he'd heard before, this voice held firm, demanding his attention. It sounded nothing like the Lord he'd begun to let in and everything like the father he'd lost as a small child.

Someone must have followed him home. Again, he scanned the room, noting the closed windows and locked front door. Finally his gaze landed on the man in the mirror.

In the dim light, he saw Brian, not himself, staring back. Frantically he tore through the Bible, looking for the tenth chapter of Romans, verse thirteen.

"For whosoever shall call upon the name of the Lord shall be saved." He closed the Bible and sat it on the mantel.

"Saved," he whispered, "from what?"

Search your heart for the answer.

"My heart." He inhaled sharply. "Brian's heart."

Realization tore through his thoughts and branded his mind with fear. Brian, the son he'd only just found, would stand a good chance of carrying the same defective gene pool as the rest of the Butlers. The breath sucked out of him in one gasp, and his knees hit the hardwood floor with an impact that should have hurt.

A pain ripped through his heart, one not physical and yet still very real. Because of him, his son could die.

"No!" he shouted, eyes lifted to the ceiling and fingers clenched into tight fists. "You took my brother and my parents. You can't have my son too!"

Pray, Luke. Call upon Me.

The voice again, now returned to the gentleness he remembered, yet still somehow firm and commanding. He took a deep breath and let it out slowly, wrapping his arms around his midsection as he allowed his eyes to shut.

"I can't," he shouted into the blackness. "I'm not like Brian and Justine. I don't even know You."

Pray, Luke. Call upon Me.

He slammed a fist against the side of the chair and sent it skittering across the slick floor. "I'm afraid," he added in a hoarse whisper.

Be not afraid.

A stroke of genius hit him. "If I'm going to turn myself over to You, there's going to be some conditions." He paused and waited for the crack of lightning he figured would strike him dead. When it didn't, he collected his thoughts and cleared his throat. "In return for my soul, Brian gets a good heart."

Silence.

"God, did You hear me?"

Again, silence.

"Okay, how about. . ."

His voice fell silent as a gentle peace tugged at the corners of his mind. Brian's face appeared, a watery image barely visible through a wash of tears.

"Okay, Lord, no deals. It's just You and me. If You want me, You've got me."

Gradually, warmth began to envelop his wounded heart, spilling into his chest and through his veins like cool water on an East Texas summer day. *Pray* came the insistent thought. *Pray and call upon Me so that you may be saved.*

And so he did.

fifteen

Justine pondered the mysteries of becoming reacquainted with Luke Butler long past the time when she should have gone inside and started dinner. She cast a quick glance at her watch, barely visible in the waning light, and frowned. Surely Brian would be famished by now, although the sounds of his work still echoed in the warm breeze.

If only the sway of the porch swing hadn't enticed her to remain outside with her thoughts, she might have seen to the task a half-hour ago. But she'd been caught up in the wonderment of seeing her son and his father together and the joy of knowing a prayer she had never thought to pray had somehow been answered all the same.

The hammering ceased, and the night grew still save for the hum of the locusts in the uppermost branches of the pecan tree. Brian would need to be fed soon. She should think of something to go with the salad she'd begun earlier, perhaps sandwiches made from the leftover roast Abby had insisted she bring home. Maybe she could stuff some baked potatoes with the roast and gravy, although that might not be what kids Brian's age considered to be a complete dinner.

She'd have to make a note to ask Abby's teenagers what sort of food to buy. Wouldn't they get a kick out of their Aunt Justine, the same aunt who could be counted on for pizza or take-out when dinnertime came around, actually thinking about cooking?

Not that cooking in any form had been on her mind

when she'd begun chopping the tomatoes and shredding the limp yellowish green lettuce. Cucumbers definitely had been the last thing she'd thought of when she began to chop the huge green prize fresh from Mildred Plotz's garden. Actually she hadn't been thinking at all. She'd been shamelessly spying on Luke and Brian, or at least she'd been trying to spy on them until her conscience got the better of her.

Slowly, she rose and stretched out the kinks in her bones. The screen door's slam broke the silence as she entered the kitchen.

"Brian?" she called. "Roast beef or baked potatoes?"

No answer.

"Brian?"

She quickened her steps as the uneasy feeling in the pit of her stomach grew. Were all mothers born with this instinct? Did God give mothers this natural feeling of concern about their children whether they raised them or not?

She practically sprinted through the living room, past the mantel where the frame of her son's picture glinted silvery white in the shadows. The night's sounds grew, and it seemed as if the locusts were crying for her, taunting her.

"Brian, where. . ."

The words died in her throat as she came to an abrupt halt. The door stood ajar, and a weak golden light spilled into the room from the front porch. Framed in the halo of brightness were Brian and his father sitting on the top step, dark heads nearly touching.

"And so it's important that you get it checked out, Son," she heard Luke say. "Just to be safe."

"Safe about what?"

Two dark heads turned, two sets of blue-green eyes regarded her with surprise. Luke looked away first, his expression unreadable, while Brian regarded her with a mixture of shock and confusion.

Instantly her "mother intuition" went on high alert. "What's going on here?"

An uneasy silence followed. Finally Luke clapped a hand on Brian's shoulder and gave him a solemn nod.

"Go on in and get cleaned up. I'll talk to your mother." He watched Brian slip past her and disappear inside before he continued. "I guess you're wondering what brings me back so soon."

She could only nod. A moth flitted inches from her head, and she ducked out of its way, then watched as it disappeared into the shadowy darkness.

"I didn't want to scare you, Justine," he began, "but I guess you'd find out sooner or later."

Her nerves danced with fear. The look he wore when he left was nowhere to be found. Instead, something akin to sadness creased his tanned face.

"Find out what?" she managed to ask.

"You know about Adam's death." Their gaze met. "And about my father's."

Again, her only response was a curt nod.

"What you don't know is that the same thing that killed them could very well take me too." He took a shuddering breath and looked past her to the closed door. "And possibly our son."

❧

Two weeks later, the conversation still shook Justine whenever she thought of it. Worse than the quiet talk around Bailey's Fork about her and Luke, worse still than the idea that Brian would be judged unfairly because of his parents, was the threat of once again losing her son, this time forever.

So as she cleared her desk of the last of her things, happiness over the good news from Luke's Houston cardiologist on Monday held prominence in her thoughts. Brian was fine.

As expected, Abby had caught on to the job of church secretary quickly, giving Justine little to do the past two weeks but watch her and worry about the men in her life. In addition to the situation with Brian and the related issue of Luke's health, her father's condition had also become worrisome.

More than once, he'd been found outside the walled courtyard of Shady Acres; twice he'd made it all the way to the parking lot. The doctors assured her that while his newfound love of roaming was indeed a problem, it might also signal some partial return to improved health. They were quick to add that improved health in no way meant the insidious disease had released its hold on his mind.

With the demands on her time increasing, Justine worried about her father and the care he so desperately needed yet could not receive at Shady Acres. Intensive one-on-one therapy could very well add quality to her father's days, if not a certain quantity to them. Services like that would be an integral part of the plans for the senior center.

Each passing day gave Justine more reason to wish the senior center would be finished in time to do her father some good. Finally, after spending what time she could manage studying the plans for the center, she would be free to oversee the details of its completion.

A few days after Luke offered her the job as director, he arrived on her doorstep with a set of plans for the now-defunct country club her father had designed three decades ago and an appetizing pasta salad. Over dinner, she had shared her vision for the facility, and together they had roughed out a design.

Her training, while not in the field of architecture, gave her a good idea of what changes were needed to adapt the facility for the seniors. Luke had passed these on to the architect in charge, then, as the project director, she had given her final approval.

In truth, she felt humbled in the presence of those who were doing the actual work. Her idea to provide a wide range of services for the area seniors had always included help, both in the building of the facility and the hiring of those who would run it. That she had been allowed to take part in the process was both an honor and a pleasure. That Luke had been an integral part of the process made things that much more rewarding.

Slowly, Justine's thoughts turned from Luke back to her father. What an irony, she thought as she closed and locked the church door for the last time. The same man who, as the lone architect in Bailey's Fork, had built the country club would now be using the building in its newest form, as a senior center.

And what an honor as his daughter to be chosen to supervise the completion of this grand endeavor. As she slid into the steamy confines of her newly repaired car and fished the keys out of her purse, Justine once again thought of Luke and smiled.

Luke Butler might not admit to lofty intentions in renovating the old country club, but she knew better. At least she thought she did.

He'd become a frequent visitor to her house over the past few weeks, often dropping by with a brown grocery sack filled with ingredients he would coax into the most amazingly wonderful meals. Doing the after-dinner cleanup together gave her ample opportunity to learn a lot about him.

"And what I don't know about Luke Butler, I'd be willing to learn," she said under her breath. Giggling like a high school girl, she cranked the engine, threw the car into gear, and headed home to await Luke and his latest creation.

Tonight they had special reason to celebrate. Brian's visit to the cardiologist showed no trace of congenital heart defects. From the corner, she could see Luke sitting on the swing, and as she turned into the driveway, she spied the familiar brown paper bags at his feet. By the time she parked in the garage, he met her with a broad smile and a bag in each hand.

"I'm sorry," she said, "it took longer than I thought to say good-bye to the old church." She reached for her purse and slid the strap over her shoulder. "I know it's just a structure and the Lord lives in the hearts of the parishioners no matter where they worship, but. . ." She paused, realizing she spoke these words to the building's new owner. Her gaze fell to the keys in her hand. "Well, I'm being silly. The new sanctuary's going to be absolutely stunning. I can't wait until Sunday."

She looked to Luke for a response and found he'd already bounded for the door. With considerably less speed, she followed him up the back steps and across the porch. Her day had been filled with last-minute meetings and minor emergencies, all conspiring to steal the joy out of an evening with her friend Luke. In an instant, his playful wink changed everything.

"You're full of energy tonight," she said as she turned the key in the lock and opened the door. "I thought you spent the afternoon at the center supervising the crew installing the new kitchen."

"I did." He closed the door with his foot and dropped the bags on the table. "I never realized how heavy those commercial ovens are." Shrugging, he reached inside the bag. "But somebody had to move them." Before she could complain, he gave her another wink. "Just kidding, Darlin', but I have been feeling exceptionally good today. Like a new man, you might say."

"That's wonderful, Luke." She kicked off her navy take-me-seriously pumps and dropped them into the basket by the back door, then tossed her keys onto the counter. "What can I do to help?"

He gave her a serious look. "Go put on your cooking clothes, Woman. Tonight *you're* making dinner."

"Me?" She feigned confusion. "You mean we're having peanut butter sandwiches?"

"*Mais non, ma chere*," he said in a poor imitation of a French accent. "Tonight you'll be making a savory creation called *Fromage Sur Canapés a la Justine avec Potage Legumes*."

She could neither make whatever this was nor pronounce it. Surely he was kidding.

"Oh Luke, how about we order pizza?" She put on her sweetest smile. "My treat."

He made a failed attempt at looking offended. "I'm going to pretend you didn't say that. Wait, what is this?" Reaching into the nearest grocery bag, he produced a clear plastic container wrapped in a black-and-white-checked dishtowel. "You're in luck, Justine, I happen to have some fresh *Potage Legumes* right here."

"But that looks like—"

Luke unwrapped the container and pretended to swipe the towel at her. "Scoot, Cook. I'm a hard-working man, and I'm hungry."

"Hey, stop that," Justine said as she scampered out of the kitchen.

By the time she'd changed from her business suit into jeans and a casual top, the music floating up through the floor told her Luke had found the CD player. Padding downstairs in her sock feet, Justine chuckled. Since when did Luke Butler like the Beatles?

She followed the music down the hall and stopped just short of the kitchen door. Luke held a stick of butter in one hand, using it as a microphone while he sang loud enough to entertain the neighbors.

Too bad he didn't sing as well as he cooked.

A moment later, Luke caught her looking. Far from being embarrassed, he upped the volume and finished the song with a bow while she applauded. With a flourish, he pressed the button and stopped the music.

"Floor show's over. Let's get down to some serious cooking." He tossed her the butter. "Ingredient number one," he said. "The rest are in the bag. Now fetch the iron skillet I bought you last week, and I'll show you what to do next."

"I don't know about this," she said. "What did you call this meal again?"

"*Fromage Sur Canapé avec Potage Legumes*." He opened the lid on the plastic container. "I need your Dutch oven to heat this."

"My what?"

"Never mind." Luke nodded toward the paper sacks, then began opening cabinet doors until he found the place where she stored her pots and pans. "Most of what we need's in the first one. The second one's got your flowers in it."

"Flowers?"

His confident smile faltered but only for a moment. "Yeah," he said, "roses." The smile returned, although his didn't quite meet her gaze.

A flush of warmth began to climb into her cheeks, and her heart inexplicably thudded against her chest. "Roses," she whispered. "Thank you," she said a bit louder.

"So put them in water, already," he said. "You've got some cooking to do."

She complied, working the unruly stems into her mother's favorite milk glass vase while her guest watched. "Now what?" she asked when the task had been completed.

"Now, you cook, but first we need a couple of things." At Luke's direction, she soon assembled an interesting selection of ingredients and utensils. Luke handed her a slice of bread, barely grazing her fingers, then dropped the butter in the pan. The faint scent of Ivory soap, whether real or imagined, floated toward her, and she nearly dropped the bread.

"Since when do you speak French?" she asked as the butter sizzled.

Luke chuckled. "Since I took a French cooking class one year in the off-season." He placed a triangle of cheese on the bread and leaned toward her. "You're doing fine. Now put the other piece on top."

She gave him a skeptical look. "What did you call this?"

"This, Darlin', is *Fromme Sur Canapé*."

"But it looks just like—"

"It is." He nudged her shoulder with his. "Are you going to cook or talk? Now grab the spatula."

Looking beyond the blue-green eyes to the task at hand, she somehow complied with Luke's instructions. Half an hour later, they sat down to the best grilled cheese sandwiches and vegetable soup she'd ever had.

"Luke," she said as she reached for her water glass, "I've been meaning to talk to you about something."

"Oh?"

She took a sip of water and returned the glass to the table. Since when had talking about the Lord become so difficult?

"I don't know where to start," she said as her heart began to race and her mouth went dry despite the water she'd just had. "So I suppose I'll just come right out and say it."

One dark brow rose as he leaned away from the table. "All right."

"I'm worried about you, Luke. I care for you, and I don't want to see you. . ." Flustered, she stared at the bowl of fruit between them. "How's your relationship with the Lord?"

"I care about you too, Justine," he said softly. "And as for me and the Big Guy, I've been working on that."

Hope soared, and she smiled in genuine relief. "You have?"

Luke returned her smile, leaning forward to extend his hand to clasp hers. "Yeah, I have." He paused. "A lot."

Something happened in that moment, an inexplicable link formed between them that went beyond their entwined fingers and entwined pasts. "I'm glad," she said. "I'd like to invite you to church this Sunday. It's the first service in the new building, and it's going to be special."

"I'll think about it." He stood abruptly. "Fetch the good bowls, Darlin'. I'm going home to get the *Sorbet aux Framboises*."

"The what?"

He dropped his napkin on the table and loped past her on the way to the door, stopping long enough to squeeze her shoulder. "Raspberry ice cream, Justine," he said.

Later, after dessert, Justine shared the photo album

Brian gave her at their first meeting, then she shared her experience of giving her life to the Lord. Luke listened to her story without comment as he poured over the pages of the book, often stopping to stare at an image of his son while he blinked back the tears. He left her with a quick hug and a promise to visit church sometime soon.

Still, the last person Justine expected to meet on the way out of the first church service in the new building was Luke Butler. Dressed like a banker but with a distinctly unbanker-like gleam in his eye, he would have been hard to miss had he been there early, so he must have slipped in late.

"What's the matter, Justine?" he whispered, linking an arm with hers as he led her down the newly paved front steps. "Cat got your tongue?"

"No. It's just that you look so. . ." Heat flamed her cheeks. "You look. . ." Words eluded her. "Oh, my," she finally stammered.

His shoulders seemed to broaden with his smile. Tilting his head in greeting to the ladies from the Clip and Curl Beauty Salon, he had the good manners to ignore their giggles and quickly return his attention to her.

"Thank you," he said simply. "And thank you for dinner last night." His smile faded. "And for sharing your faith with me. It meant a lot."

She tried not to show her surprise. "It did?"

Another nod and they fell into silence. Rounding the corner to the parking lot, they came face to face with Dan Mills.

"Good morning, Dan," Luke said, much of his familiar cheerfulness returning. "Great sermon. Thank you."

This morning's message, much like the one the week before, had drawn heavily from the gospels of Matthew and Luke. The parallel between the theme presented on Sunday and the spectacle that took place between her and Luke on First Street a little more than a month ago had been hard to miss. Christians are called to practice forgiveness and unconditional love, Pastor Mills had declared from his pulpit.

Justine had thanked him privately last week, her heart light with the results the single sermon had brought. Today's addition would hopefully bring the wagging tongues to a halt, or at least silence them for the most part.

Brian deserved as much, even if she and Luke did not.

While the pastor engaged Luke in conversation about the soon-to-be-completed senior center, Justine eyed the distance to her car. Last night she'd managed to concentrate first on cooking, then on Brian and the pictures they poured over together. Long after Luke had gone home, memories of the evening left her thoughts spinning in directions she preferred not to go. Spending five minutes on the sidewalk outside the new Bailey's Fork Community Church had the same effect.

And as nice as it felt, she knew it was wrong to allow it to continue.

Somewhere between the light and delicious seafood crepes on Monday, the authentic Sicilian pasta primavera with pesto and garlic on Thursday, and last night's grilled cheese sandwiches, she'd begun to think of Luke as more than just a guy from her past. He'd become something indefinable, someone important for more than just his contribution to their son's gene pool. If she weren't careful, she just might figure out how she felt.

A tug on her elbow brought her focus back to the present, where Luke beamed at her like a kid with a new bicycle. "Isn't that right, Darlin'?" he asked.

"I'm sorry," she stammered. "I guess I wasn't paying attention."

Luke shrugged and cast a sideways glance at the pastor, who shook his head and wished them a quick good-bye. As Justine watched Dan Mills walk away, she heard Luke clear his throat.

"I'd like you to take a ride with me," he said slowly. "If you will, that is."

"A ride?" Justine stared past him to where her car sat waiting in the shade. "Thanks, but my car's out of the shop. See?" She gestured toward the car. "I sure was lucky to get a spot in the shade, especially since—"

"C'mon, Justine, humor me."

She stared past him to the shady spot where her car beckoned. "Why?"

He seemed at a loss for an answer. Red flags went up, and she began to wonder if her sister had told him today was her birthday.

Surely Abby wouldn't have mentioned it. Not after the discussion she'd had with her.

"On my honor, I promise," Abby had said, and Justine had been left with no reason not to believe her.

Luke whirled her around and gently aimed her in the opposite direction from her vehicle. Without a word, he caught her elbow and steered her across the lawn and around the corner, where a shiny black four-wheel drive SUV waited by the curb.

"Where's your Harley?" she asked as he gallantly opened the door and helped her inside. The smell of leather assailed her nose and made her sneeze.

"God bless you," he said as he took his place in the driver's seat and closed the door. "And to answer your question, the Harley's at home." He gave her a quick up-and-down look. "I didn't think you'd be dressed for a motorcycle ride."

Justine smoothed the hem of her skirt down over her knees and tried to make sense of her reeling thoughts. "Where are we going?" she finally thought to ask after they'd traveled a few miles down the highway.

He answered with a nod as he signaled and slowed the vehicle to turn. "We're already here."

Justine stared with amazement as Luke brought the vehicle to a stop in the parking lot of Shady Acres. Words sprung to her throat, but her lips somehow failed to form them.

Before she could remedy the situation, Luke shifted positions to take both her hands in his. Their eyes met and locked, and a thousand butterflies fluttered in her stomach.

"Justine, I came back to Bailey's Fork with trouble in mind, and trouble's just what I found." He mustered a wry smile. "Only it wasn't the kind I expected."

Still the words would not come. She answered with a smile of her own.

"I think you may have guessed that I've been finding ways to spend an awful lot of time with you lately," he said softly. "I'm just not sure you realize it's been real hard to be alone with you. Last night I had to invent a trip home for ice cream to keep from kissing you."

"Why?" Her voice cracked with emotion.

"Because what I want to do and what the Lord tells me I ought to do are two different things."

Justine swallowed hard. Had she heard him right? Why hadn't he mentioned this last night?

Squeezing her fingers softly, Luke raised them to his lips. "I'm a changed man, Justine," he said slowly. "A saved man."

"Oh, Luke," she whispered in a rush of happiness as she fell into his embrace. "How? When? Did you feel this way last night? I mean, you seemed different, happier, I guess, and so full of life. Is that what happened?"

His chuckle rumbled deep in his chest and shook her. "You're sure asking a lot of questions, Darlin'." He pulled back to hold her at arm's length. "And I intend to answer every one of them. But right now I need to do something."

Despite the wonderful, frightening, surprising tangle of emotions surging through her, she managed to ask, "What's that?"

"This," he whispered.

Then he kissed her.

Too soon, he ended the soft mingling of their lips. "Let's go," he said, opening the door.

"Go?" She'd nearly forgotten where they were. Slowly, as Luke rounded the front of the vehicle and reached to open the door and help her out, the realization returned.

"Luke, what're you up to?" She watched him disappear through the all-too-familiar front doors of the nursing home.

He shortened his stride to allow her to catch up, then wrapped an arm around her shoulder. For a moment, in Luke's protective embrace, the world and all its unpleasant realities receded, leaving only the two of them.

"I have to make things right with your father, Justine," he said, determination lighting his eyes.

"But he'll never understand. He probably won't even know who you are." She bit her lip and looked away. "Maybe this isn't such a good idea."

Luke cradled her chin in the palm of his hand and gently turned her face toward him. "Justine, if I'm ever going to be the man your father wanted me to be, I've got to do this."

She blinked back the tears shimmering beneath her lashes and simply nodded. Slowly, she took his hand. "I understand," she whispered.

sixteen

The electric door slid shut behind Justine, and she stepped into the world of Shady Acres. Unlike the county hospital where her father was an all-too-frequent visitor, this place stood as silent as a tomb, and it never failed to unnerve her. Only the occasional closing of a door or ring of a telephone marred the perfect peace. On more than one occasion, Justine had fought the urge to make some sort of joyful noise or cartwheel down the hallways just to shake things up a bit.

The weekend charge nurse, a petite woman who looked more like a resident than an employee, looked up from her work and offered a smile. "Well, hello there, Miss Kane, Mr. Butler," she said slowly. "Nice afternoon for a visit, isn't it?"

Justine returned the greeting, then stopped and leveled a hand at Luke's chest. "How does she know your name?" she asked.

He shrugged, looking anything but innocent as he gave the nurse a wink before he set off down the first hall to the right. "Must be a football fan," he said over his shoulder.

Their footsteps echoed down the wide corridor and beat a rapid cadence, matching the one Justine's heart had found. "Up there," she whispered. "His is the next to last one on the left. Two doors from the dining room."

A few steps shy of her father's room, Justine stopped short. She cast a long glance at the closed door and took a deep breath, releasing it slowly.

"This is a really bad idea, Luke. I just know it."

Luke regarded her with mild curiosity as he straightened his tie. "Probably," he said with a nod of his head. "And so is this."

Without warning, he lowered his lips to hers and gave her a quick kiss. Before she could catch her breath or even attempt a response, Luke caught her by the wrist and led her down the hall, past her father's door.

"Hey wait a minute. He's back there."

"No, Darlin'," Luke said. "He's right here." Slowly, Luke released his hold on her. "Happy birthday," he whispered.

She followed his broad back through the double doors and into the dining room, where yards of red, blue, yellow, and green crepe paper had been strewn across the wide bank of windows on the opposite wall. A giant sign wishing her a happy birthday in bright red letters hung suspended from the ceiling in the center of the room. Little notes were scribbled all over it, each one signed. Someone, most likely Abby, had blown up Justine's second-grade picture, the one where she forgot to tell her mother it was picture day, and tacked it to the bottom of the sign.

Beneath the silly picture sat her father in his favorite red chair flanked by an assortment of friends and family members. Brian kneeled at his grandfather's elbow with Becky beside him. Even the mayor and Pastor Mills were there with their wives, and Officer Eli Watts stood off to one side with his brother. On the count of three, they all began to sing "Happy Birthday" to her.

Even her father.

"Daddy," she said under her breath as she watched him struggle to his feet with the aid of his walking cane and a little help from his eldest grandson. She turned to look at Luke through a shimmering of tears. "How did you manage. . .this?"

Her gaze shifted to Abby. Before she could say a word, her sister shook her head and held up both hands.

"Don't look at me, Justine. I didn't say a word. Luke thought of this on his own."

Again she faced Luke. "You did this for me?"

He nodded and took both her hands in his just as he had done earlier in the car. Lifting them to his lips once more, he smiled as a cheer went up from the crowd.

Too soon he let go and leaned toward her. "All that's for you," he said in soft whispers that sent shivers up and down her spine. "But this is for me."

Without a word of warning, he strode purposefully toward her father. The crowd fell silent when Luke offered his hand to Arthur Kane.

"Sir," he said in a clear, controlled voice. "Do you know who I am?"

Abby started to speak, but Hank silenced her with a look. Justine bit her lip and swiped at her tears with the back of her hand.

For an eternity, her father said nothing. Justine held her breath. Some days were better than others with the elder Kane, but most days weren't very good at all. The last three times she'd come to visit, he'd ignored her completely. The doctors suspected a stroke.

She took a deep breath and began to pray that the Lord would allow her father a clear mind, if only for a few minutes. As if he were moving in slow motion, her father's hand began to rise, finally making contact with Luke's. Recognition glimmered in his wrinkled face; then, as had happened so many times in the past, it died away to leave him looking confused, angry. To her amazement, he neither moved nor released his hand from Luke's, but merely stood tall and proud, staring eye to eye with him.

"Butler," he said slowly, his brows creasing to a deep furrow. "Luke."

Abby gasped, and through the tears that now fell freely, Justine saw Hank take his fiancée's hand.

"Yes, Sir," Luke said, his spine straight as a steel rod. "That's right."

Her father's left shoulder sank a bit, but he stood firm. "What?" he began, then stopped and shook his head. "Why. . . ?"

"I made some mistakes the first time around, Sir, and I'm here to see it doesn't happen again." An edge of defiance tempered the softness in his deep voice. He cleared his throat. "I'm not the man I used to be, and I don't mind admitting it."

Her father shook his head and pulled his hand away from Luke. Brian steadied his grandfather by moving to stand directly behind him. He was a head taller but just as proud; Justine noticed a tear trickle down her son's face, and it was all she could do not to wipe it away.

"No," the elder man continued. "I. . .mistakes. . .me. . ." He shook his head as if he knew what he'd said hadn't made much sense, and Justine's heart nearly broke.

Brian patted his grandfather's shoulder. "It's okay, Paw Paw," he said gently.

"No, not," he responded, focusing his gaze on Justine. Slowly, he said her name, drawing the syllables out like a child testing his voice for the first time.

"Yes, Daddy," she somehow managed as she gave silent thanks to the Lord for her birthday miracle. "It's me."

He, too, had adopted a proud stance, and from where she stood, he almost looked like the father she remembered, the one she knew before the awful disease had taken hold. Before she realized she'd done it, Justine crossed the room to take him in her arms. To her great surprise, he returned the embrace with a strength she had no idea he still possessed. Brian's arms snaked around both of them and held them for a moment.

Too soon, her father pulled away to face Luke. For a brief moment, Justine thought she saw a glimpse of the old Kane determination and possibly anger.

"Butler," he said harshly.

Luke dipped his head slightly in deference but kept his posture rigid, his shoulders squared. "Yes, Sir."

"Ask," he said slowly, his eyes never leaving Luke.

Blinking hard, Luke took a deep breath and let it out slowly. He took hold of Justine's hand and held it tight as he faced Arthur Kane the same way he had nearly twenty years ago.

"If you tell me no, I'll respect your wishes this time, Sir. And if you tell me yes, I'll be happier than the day I rushed for three hundred yards and made four touchdowns in the Pro Bowl." He squeezed Justine's hand and studied the toes of his black loafers for a long moment. "Mr. Kane, what I mean to say is, I'd like to ask permission to see your daughter," he said in a determined voice. "To date her properly and for as long as she'll put up with me."

Abby gasped, while Justine began to cry in earnest. Brian gave a soft cheer and patted his grandfather's shoulder. A few murmurs from the assembled crowd were the only other signs of life in the room for what seemed like an eternity.

Her father studied Luke, then swung his gaze in her direction for a fraction of a second. Justine began to pray, giving thanks, asking for guidance, and requesting strength to accept whatever happened.

Finally, Arthur Kane nodded. "Yes," he added for

emphasis as he sank into his chair with a crooked smile while the rest of the party guests erupted in shouts of joy.

❧

Long after the cake had been consumed and the punch bowl had been drained, Justine and Luke stood beneath the handmade sign with the awful picture. Arthur Kane's big afternoon had been a success, and Luke's gallant words to him had mended more than just one heart. Now, in the silence of the empty room, Justine felt no need to say more.

Wrapped in Luke's arms, she could have stayed forever. Too soon, though, the cleaning crew shooed them out to prepare the room for the evening meal. Practically floating, she followed Luke down the hall and out to the parking lot.

"I've got a little something for you," Luke said when they'd returned to the car. He fished behind the seat and retrieved a small box wrapped in silver paper. "Happy birthday."

"You didn't have to do this, Luke," Justine said. "The party, my father, all of that was so much more than I ever expected."

"Open it, Darlin'." He paused and looked unsure of himself. "If you don't like it, I don't think I can take it back."

Justine wasted no time unwrapping the paper, then paused when she saw the green velvet box. A ring box. Was she ready for this? What would she say?

The old feelings she'd once had for Luke had all come tumbling back in the past month, along with some new ones she'd never expected. Always, when she thought of him, she rejected the possibility of a life together because of his beliefs.

But now, given his claim earlier today, did she still feel there could be nothing between them? One long look into his blue-green eyes, and she fell headlong into a love she'd been running from for twenty years.

"Oh, Luke, thank you," she whispered as she gently opened the box. "Luke, what is this?" she asked when the gold key fell into her lap.

"The Greater Gifts," he said with a smile. "Buckle up, and I'll show you what I'm talking about."

A few minutes later, Luke pulled the big black vehicle to a stop in front of the old church building, the same one where he'd stumbled upon her packing away hymnals in the attic. Someone had removed the original sign marking the red brick structure as the home of Bailey's Fork Community Church. In its place hung a hand-lettered sign with the words "The Greater Gifts" written in bold red script, the same script as her birthday sign.

"What is this?" she asked as he helped her out of the car.

"It's yours," he said.

"Mine? The old church building?" She shook her head. "I don't understand."

He took the key from her hand and crossed the sidewalk to fit it into the ancient lock. The carved oak doors creaked in protest when he swung them open and disappeared inside. Slowly, she followed.

"I'm in here. Come sit with me, Darlin'."

His voice seemed to have come from the chapel, so she followed it there but stopped short when she crossed the threshold. Rarely in her job as church secretary had Justine been called to visit the sanctuary in late afternoon, and certainly she had never seen the old room glow with the fire of a thousand points of light as it did now.

Luke seemed to be at the center of the lights, his image diffused with the brilliance of the many colors the sun made as it shone through the old stained glass panels and the watery shimmering of her tears. Silly, she thought, that a sunlit room on a Sunday afternoon could bring her to the point of weeping.

"Come sit with me," Luke said again.

They settled together in the front pew and sat in silence a few moments. "So beautiful," he whispered as he turned to wipe a stray tear from her cheek with the back of his hand. "There's so much I want to tell you."

Justine managed a smile. "I've got all day," she said slowly.

He nodded and looked away. "How do you like having Brian around the house?"

"It's great," she said. "Although between the work you've got him doing at the center and the time he spends on the phone with Becky, I'm afraid the only time I see him is at mealtimes and at church on Sunday."

Luke expelled a long breath and took her hand in his, studying her fingers while he seemed to collect his thoughts. "I told you I was a changed man earlier. I didn't tell you why or how," he said slowly. "It all started the day I found out about Brian."

"Oh."

"Yeah." He squeezed her hand. "The Lord really got my attention that day, although I've got to tell you I fought Him pretty hard. Eventually I made a deal with Him, though."

Justine suppressed a smile. "A deal? Luke, we don't make deals with the heavenly Father. It's just not done."

"I know that now, but I didn't know it then. I told Him if He would heal my boy, I was His." He lifted her fingers to his lips in a now-familiar gesture, then smiled. "He took me up on the offer, and I turned my life over to Him. The bonus is that I got made new too." He released her fingers and thumped his chest. "The doctors can't explain it, but I know how it happened."

She shook her head. "What're you talking about? When did you see a doctor?"

"Brian and I went together. I asked him not to say anything to you because you had enough on your mind worrying about him." He threw his head back and laughed. "I sure fooled those medical types when all my tests came out negative and my heart looked like it belonged to a guy half my age. They're still trying to figure out what happened to the genetic heart disease I was supposed to have."

"But. . ." Tears began to fall again, and the lump in her throat stalled any further conversation.

"I know," he said gently. "God planned this all along, but I'm still getting used to it."

" 'A man's heart deviseth his way: but the Lord directeth his steps.' " Justine offered a shy smile. "The story of our lives, I'm afraid. Yours and mine."

Silence gathered around them as he held her and wiped away each tear before it fell. Finally he kissed her wet cheek. "The senior center's almost done. Another couple of months and we can apply for state certification. After that, you're going to be out of work."

The abrupt change in conversation stunned her. Slowly she made sense of what he'd said, and her heart sunk. Did Luke actually expect her to walk away from the project after the renovations were done?

"I thought I might volunteer there," she said. "Maybe dust off my diploma and do some real counseling work."

Luke nodded again. "I had the same thought, about the counseling, I mean." His gaze returned to her. "But I thought there might be another place for you to do it."

"Where?"

His smile lit the room and warmed her heart. "Here."

"I don't follow you."

He stood and pulled her to her feet. "You're amazing, you know? What you did. For Brian, I mean." He took a few steps down the carpeted aisle, and she followed. "You were able to give him away because it was the best thing for him." Abruptly he turned to face her. "Not everyone could have made that sacrifice."

She opened her mouth to speak, but he silenced her with a finger to her lips. His eyes danced, and the happiness she saw there felt almost contagious. Still, confusion clouded her happiness.

"What does that have to do with all this?"

"I think you could help others who are in the same situation, Justine." He smiled. "I'd like you to use your diploma and this building to help kids like you. Like us."

"What're you saying, Luke?"

"I'm saying this county needs someone willing to help. Someone who can teach job skills classes, counsel those who need it, and maybe even offer some sort of interim child care while they get on their feet again." He expelled a deep breath. "I want The Greater Gifts Foundation to do whatever it takes to help a family stay together."

Family.

Justine attempted to absorb Luke's words. How wonderful it would be if it were possible to help, to counsel girls like her. To give them a choice where she had none.

But could she do it? Silently she searched her heart, then asked the Lord.

Yes, Justine, you can do it, was the answer her heart heard.

seventeen

One year later

"I can do this paperwork and have lunch too," Justine said softly. "Care to join me?"

Brian shook his head. "Can't. Uncle Hank asked me to deliver this to Dad ASAP. Now that he's got the Lakeside retreat open, I'm pretty much the whole staff at the delivery service."

She began to unwrap the container. "Has Hank decided what he's going to do for a staff when you go back to college in the fall?"

"He said he's thinking of selling out to the Watts brothers."

"Eli and Zeke?" She retrieved a napkin from the paper sack and placed it in her lap. "I didn't know they were in the market for a career change."

"Don't ask me," Brian said. "Where did you say my dad was?"

Justine shifted the mountain of paperwork to one side and cleared a spot on her desk. "He's helping me with the four and five year olds. Our preschool teacher had a dentist appointment, and I'm supposed to meet a documentary crew in half an hour."

"A documentary. Cool. When did this happen?"

Justine shrugged and fished inside the bag for a plastic fork. "I got the call this morning."

She took a bite of chicken salad from the newly reopened First Street Bakery and Deli and chewed slowly.

The bakery, located on the site of the original one, had opened three weeks ago. While some attributed the standing-room-only crowds at lunch and dinner Tuesdays through Saturdays to Luke's fame as a former football player, Justine knew it had to be his talent in the kitchen.

"Oh, wow, this is good," she said slowly. "Mine never tastes like this. How does he do it?"

"He said the secret's in the marinating." Brian shrugged, then shifted the package he held in his arms. "Whatever that means. Hey, I gotta go."

"Sure, Sweetheart." She reached for another taste. "Tell your father he's outdone himself this time."

Brian stepped out of the office and returned a few minutes later. "Um, Mom, do you mind taking this to Dad?" He pointed to the cellular phone hanging from his belt. "Delivery emergency. You understand." Without waiting for an answer, he tossed the package on the corner of the desk and beat a hasty retreat. "Thanks, Mom," echoed down the hall, followed by the distant slamming of a door.

"Delivery emergency?"

Justine stuffed another scrumptious bite into her mouth, then retrieved the package and headed for the upstairs classroom where the four and five year olds were busy practicing the alphabet.

So many changes had occurred in the year since Luke handed her the key to The Greater Gifts Foundation. The old church building had been renovated and almost immediately the line for those needing help had stretched around the block. Patience, persistence, and strong reliance on the Lord helped Justine handle the difficult early days. All of these things plus her growing love for Luke kept the foundation expanding.

No matter what the job, Luke always seemed willing to

pitch in and help. It had been his ability to feed a crowd on short notice that gave him the idea to reopen the First Street Bakery.

After two bites, she had no doubt his latest masterpiece, chicken salad with red grapes and slivered almonds, would go far to keep it in business. Of course, she thought that about every dish he asked her to sample.

Justine arrived at the door to the classroom, the package tucked under her arm. A squeal of delight and a round of laughter from inside the room made her pause to peek through the window.

Inside, Luke sat in the center of the bright blue carpet, seven laughing children dancing in circles around him. On his head, he wore a crown. When he saw her, he broke into a broad grin.

"Look, kids," she heard him announce. "It's Miss Kane."

The children continued to hop and skip and generally move about, even though Luke stood and slipped out of the circle to walk toward her.

"What are you doing?" she asked with a giggle.

His smile broadened. "We're making a joyful noise unto the Lord."

Before she could protest, Luke gave her a quick kiss on the cheek, sending the group into fits of laughter. "Pipe down, Munchkins," he teased over his shoulder. "Can't a guy greet his girl?"

His girl.

The words warmed her heart and coaxed a smile when she'd intended to scold him for not following the lesson plan. Oh yes, she thought, as she watched Luke wade back into the center of the circle, there were much worse things than being known as Luke Butler's girl.

Even at the ripe old age of thirty-seven. Thirty-eight

tomorrow, she corrected, as she dropped the package on the nearest table.

A glint of silver brought her attention to the foil crown perched askance on his dark head. "Why are you wearing that?" she asked.

Ignoring her question, he clapped his hands, bringing the merrymaking to a quick halt. "It's time," he announced.

"Time for what?"

Justine watched in amazement as each of the kids settled beside Luke without protest. The last time she'd attempted to corral this class, she'd lost one girl and two boys, only to find them later in the sanctuary drawing on the walls with colored chalk.

"Time to show you what we did with our alphabet project," he said with a smug look. "I'll bet you thought all we did was party around here." Another round of giggles got quickly suppressed with a look of mock anger from Luke. "Okay, kids, it's show time. Close your eyes, Miss Kane."

"I don't think this is a good idea."

Luke turned to the children and shook his head. "What did I tell you? She's no fun."

"I am too," Justine protested. "It's just—"

"No fun," the children echoed in unison.

"Okay, but only if I get to wear the crown," she said.

"Oh, Darlin', I was hoping you'd say that."

He lifted the crown off his head and placed it on hers, making a big fuss of adjusting it to sit just so. His lips gently touched her eyes, closing them. Two strong hands pushed her down until she sank into a child-sized chair.

All at once, the group must have dispersed, because it sounded as if a small herd of elephants had been unleashed in the classroom. When she opened her eyes, each child had returned to his or her position on the rug. In front of each of them lay a plain white poster board. Every one of them, including Luke, looked as if they were about to do something they would be scolded for later.

"Okay, remember how we did it in rehearsal," Luke said.

"Rehearsal? I don't remember anything in the lesson plan about a rehearsal."

He touched a finger to her lips. "Just enjoy," he whispered. "And remember I love you."

I love you.

As long as she lived she would never tire of hearing him say those words. "Thank You, Lord," she whispered to heaven, "for Luke Butler."

Luke dropped to one knee beside her and gave the signal. "Ready, set, go!"

The first child, a shy redheaded girl who'd only been with the program a short time, surprised Justine by holding her poster board up first. "Will," she said, reading the word written in a childish scrawl.

The next child, the same feisty girl who had led the boys in the unfortunate chalk incident, held hers aloft. Upside down, Justine could barely make out the word written there. "You," the girl said with a giggle.

In rapid succession, each child lifted his or her poster board until all the words were showing. Only then did Justine make sense of it all. Tears, her constant companions during just about any occasion, began to flow.

"Read it out loud, Mom."

She whirled around to find Brian standing in the doorway. Behind him it seemed half of Bailey's Fork had crowded into the hall. Justine turned to Luke and smiled through the sheen of tears.

"What's the matter, Darlin'," he asked slowly. "Cat got your tongue?"

Somehow she managed to shake her head.

"Then do as the boy says and read it." He gestured behind her. "Better make it loud, though. For the cameras."

"Cameras?" She turned to see the documentary crew she'd been expecting. "Oh, Luke," she whispered.

Luke feigned impatience. "If Miss Kane's not going to read, I guess we'll all have to do it together, won't we, kids?"

They squealed with laughter, then instantly quieted when Luke gave the signal.

Suddenly, the room filled with the voices of seven happy, fidgeting children and one adult male whose voice seemed to crack halfway through. "Will you marry me, Miss Kane?" they shouted in unison.

Of course, after she adjusted her silver crown, she said yes.

LUKE BUTLER'S FIRST STREET BAKERY AND DELI CHICKEN SALAD

Ingredients:
1 whole chicken
1 package dry Italian dressing mix
1 cup chopped red grapes
½ cup chopped celery
1 cup slivered almonds
½ to 1 cup mayonnaise

Boil chicken, cool, and chop. Prepare dressing mix according to package directions and pour over chicken. Refrigerate overnight. Drain any excess and add grapes, celery, and almonds. Add mayonnaise to taste and serve.

A Letter To Our Readers

Dear Reader:

In order that we might better contribute to your reading enjoyment, we would appreciate your taking a few minutes to respond to the following questions. We welcome your comments and read each form and letter we receive. When completed, please return to the following:

Rebecca Germany, Fiction Editor
Heartsong Presents
PO Box 719
Uhrichsville, Ohio 44683

1. Did you enjoy reading *You Can't Buy Love* by Kathleen Y'Barbo?

   ❑ Very much! I would like to see more books by this author!

   ❑ Moderately. I would have enjoyed it more if

   ____

   ____

2. Are you a member of **Heartsong Presents**? Yes ❑ No ❑
   If no, where did you purchase this book?______________

   ____

3. How would you rate, on a scale from 1 (poor) to 5 (superior), the cover design?______________________________

4. On a scale from 1 (poor) to 10 (superior), please rate the following elements.

   _____ Heroine _____ Plot

   _____ Hero _____ Inspirational theme

   _____ Setting _____ Secondary characters

5. These characters were special because______________

____

____

6. How has this book inspired your life?______________

____

____

7. What settings would you like to see covered in future **Heartsong Presents** books?______________________

____

____

8. What are some inspirational themes you would like to see treated in future books?______________________

____

____

9. Would you be interested in reading other **Heartsong Presents** titles? Yes ❑ No ❑

10. Please check your age range:

❑ Under 18 ❑ 18-24 ❑ 25-34

❑ 35-45 ❑ 46-55 ❑ Over 55

Name ____

Occupation ______________________________________

Address ____

City ______________ State __________ Zip __________

Email ____

South Carolina

The female instinct to protect and provide for her family is strong. But can these four Southern women stand up to the challenges that rage against their loved ones?

The ultimate family man is God—but will each of these women turn to Him for counsel? Can they comprehend His lessons on true love?

Contemporary, paperback, 464 pages, 5 3⁄16" x 8"

♥ ♥ ♥ ♥ ♥ ♥ ♥ ♥ ♥ ♥ ♥ ♥ ♥ ♥ ♥ ♥ ♥

Please send me ____ copies of *South Carolina*. I am enclosing $5.97 for each. (Please add $2.00 to cover postage and handling per order. OH add 6% tax.)

Send check or money order, no cash or C.O.D.s please.

Name____

Address______________________________________

City, State, Zip ________________________________

To place a credit card order, call 1-800-847-8270.

Send to: Heartsong Presents Reader Service, PO Box 721, Uhrichsville, OH 44683

♥ ♥ ♥ ♥ ♥ ♥ ♥ ♥ ♥ ♥ ♥ ♥ ♥ ♥ ♥ ♥ ♥

Heartsong

CONTEMPORARY ROMANCE IS CHEAPER BY THE DOZEN!

Buy any assortment of twelve *Heartsong Presents* titles and save 25% off of the already discounted price of $2.95 each!

*plus $2.00 shipping and handling per order and sales tax where applicable.

HEARTSONG PRESENTS *TITLES AVAILABLE NOW:*

__HP177 NEPALI NOON, *S. Hayden*
__HP178 EAGLES FOR ANNA, *C. Runyon*
__HP181 RETREAT TO LOVE, *N. Rue*
__HP182 A WING AND A PRAYER, *T. Peterson*
__HP186 WINGS LIKE EAGLES, *T. Peterson*
__HP189 A KINDLED SPARK, *C. Reece*
__HP193 COMPASSIONATE LOVE, *A. Bell*
__HP194 WAIT FOR THE MORNING, *K. Baez*
__HP197 EAGLE PILOT, *J. Stengl*
__HP201 A WHOLE NEW WORLD, *Y. Lehman*
__HP205 A QUESTION OF BALANCE, *V. B. Jones*
__HP206 POLITICALLY CORRECT, *K. Cornelius*
__HP209 SOFT BEATS MY HEART, *A. Carter*
__HP210 THE FRUIT OF HER HANDS, *J. Orcutt*
__HP213 PICTURE OF LOVE, *T. H. Murray*
__HP214 TOMORROW'S RAINBOW, *V. Wiggins*
__HP217 ODYSSEY OF LOVE, *M. Panagiotopoulos*
__HP218 HAWAIIAN HEARTBEAT, *Y.Lehman*
__HP221 THIEF OF MY HEART, *C. Bach*
__HP222 FINALLY, LOVE, *J. Stengl*
__HP225 A ROSE IS A ROSE, *R. R. Jones*
__HP226 WINGS OF THE DAWN, *T. Peterson*
__HP233 FAITH CAME LATE, *F. Chrisman*
__HP234 GLOWING EMBERS, *C. L. Reece*
__HP237 THE NEIGHBOR, *D. W. Smith*
__HP238 ANNIE'S SONG, *A. Boeshaar*
__HP242 FAR ABOVE RUBIES, *B. Melby and C. Wienke*
__HP245 CROSSROADS, *T. and J. Peterson*
__HP246 BRIANNA'S PARDON, *G. Clover*
__HP254 THE REFUGE, *R. Simons*
__HP261 RACE OF LOVE, *M. Panagiotopoulos*
__HP262 HEAVEN'S CHILD, *G. Fields*
__HP265 HEARTH OF FIRE, *C. L. Reece*
__HP266 WHAT LOVE REMEMBERS, *M. G. Chapman*
__HP269 WALKING THE DOG, *G. Sattler*
__HP270 PROMISE ME FOREVER, *A. Boeshaar*
__HP273 SUMMER PLACE, *P. Darty*
__HP274 THE HEALING PROMISE, *H. Alexander*
__HP277 ONCE MORE WITH FEELING, *B. Bancroft*
__HP278 ELIZABETH'S CHOICE, *L. Lyle*
__HP282 THE WEDDING WISH, *L. Lough*
__HP289 THE PERFECT WIFE, *G. Fields*
__HP297 A THOUSAND HILLS, *R. McCollum*
__HP298 A SENSE OF BELONGING, *T. Fowler*
__HP302 SEASONS, *G. G. Martin*
__HP305 CALL OF THE MOUNTAIN, *Y. Lehman*
__HP306 PIANO LESSONS, *G. Sattler*
__HP310 THE RELUCTANT BRIDE, *H. Spears*
__HP317 LOVE REMEMBERED, *A. Bell*
__HP318 BORN FOR THIS LOVE, *B. Bancroft*
__HP321 FORTRESS OF LOVE, *M. Panagiotopoulos*
__HP322 COUNTRY CHARM, *D. Mills*
__HP325 GONE CAMPING, *G. Sattler*
__HP326 A TENDER MELODY, *B. L. Etchison*
__HP329 MEET MY SISTER, TESS, *K. Billerbeck*
__HP330 DREAMING OF CASTLES, *G. G. Martin*
__HP337 OZARK SUNRISE, *H. Alexander*
__HP338 SOMEWHERE A RAINBOW, *Y. Lehman*
__HP341 IT ONLY TAKES A SPARK, *P. K. Tracy*
__HP342 THE HAVEN OF REST, *A. Boeshaar*
__HP346 DOUBLE TAKE, *T. Fowler*
__HP349 WILD TIGER WIND, *G. Buck*
__HP350 RACE FOR THE ROSES, *L. Snelling*
__HP353 ICE CASTLE, *J. Livingston*
__HP354 FINDING COURTNEY, *B. L. Etchison*
__HP357 WHITER THAN SNOW, *Y. Lehman*

(If ordering from this page, please remember to include it with the order form.)